A HOUSE SHARED

ADAM GANT
AND PATRICIA NICHOLSON

On the significance of the four point star:

It's the Northern Star,
   the Guiding Star,
      and the Wishing Star.

It's always been a sign of hope for all the
dreamers working towards a brighter future.

INSIGHTFUL BOOKS FIRST EDITION, JUNE 2020

*Copyright © 2020 by Adam Gant
and Patricia Nicholson
Graphics Copyright © 2020 Michelle Fairbanks*

Published in North America by Insightful Books, a division of 1086353 BC Ltd., Vancouver, British Columbia, Canada. This complete edition was originally published in 2020.

Insightful Books is a trademark

ISBN: 978-1-7772796-0-8

Cover Art Design by Michelle Fairbanks

Printed in Canada

For anyone who has ever wanted
to own more real estate.

A House Shared

Table of Contents

PART ONE
Present Day

Chapter 1
SHOTGUN

Kevin Robertson kept looking at the message on his phone for a few seconds after he'd finished reading it. It had been a long time since he'd heard news of Ralph Heinz, the first big investor to partner with him on the software business that had christened his business career. It sent his thoughts back 22 years, to the moment when Ralph's actions had locked Kevin's life onto a roller coaster trajectory. That experience had toughened him, but he hadn't thought about it very often in the last few years. There was a time when a day wouldn't go by without Kevin wondering what Ralph must have been doing or thinking in the week leading up to his attack on Kevin's company.

Kevin would picture Ralph lingering a little longer than usual over breakfast while mentally rehearsing the steps of his Machiavellian plan. Kevin remembered being so stunned by Ralph's actions that it felt like being hit with a sledge hammer, but to Ralph it was probably like any other day at the office.

Ralph must have spent several days reviewing and considering the shareholders' agreement that he and Kevin had signed for Matterhorn Cryptography Corp., the cybersecurity software company Kevin founded. The name came from the inspiration Kevin had to start the business during a trip to Switzerland to climb the Matterhorn mountain with friends. The company got off to a good start and had grown fast right out of the gate. Kevin believed they had met all of the investors' expectations and were still on track to keep growing which is why it was so shocking when Ralph decided to trigger the shotgun clause. Kevin would later learn that this wasn't the first time Ralph had used a shotgun clause to acquire control of a company. Nor was it Ralph's first time taking activist measures to exert his will over the people he was in business with.

Ralph Heinz was 62 years old at the time but Kevin remembered Ralph saying to anyone who asked that he would still be working well into his 70s. Most who knew him believed it. He seemed to like building his stake in companies as a way to keep score. From what Kevin understood of his financial status at the time, Ralph didn't need to work anymore to enjoy a comfortable retirement.

It was so long ago that it was hard to know for sure, but Kevin thought Ralph must have been driven by a deeply seated fear of poverty. Ralph had told him stories during a rare lunch meeting, that hunger had been a recurring fixture of his childhood, receding for a while only to return the next time his father was out of work. As a young man, he had been determined never to experience that again. Decades later, it was probably no longer a conscious motivation, but Kevin guessed it still drove Ralph's lifelong need to put as much distance between himself and those memories.

Kevin wondered if Ralph would say he looked forward to "firing" the shotgun. Ralph seemed like the kind of person who believed that no matter what happened, things would ultimately go his way and he always seemed prepared with alternatives.

Given the way Kevin received the documents that day and the timing of when they were delivered, Ralph's lawyer, Greg, must have been working on it days in advance. As a strategy, a shotgun clause was like going "all-in" near the end of a poker game to force your opponent to make a tough decision. When one shareholder wants to take over complete ownership of a company, they can trigger a shotgun clause with their partners. With a shotgun offer, the other person had to either accept the buyout and walk away or they would have to match the offer and buy out the offering party at that same price. It was clear that Ralph had wanted control of the company but knowing his distaste for paying a premium he had probably calculated the lowest possible price he could offer that would still be enough to force Kevin out. If Ralph had offered too little, however, it would have been easier for Kevin to find new partners to match his offer and buy him out.

In this case, because Ralph's end goal was to own more of the company, he had to offer enough to make it hard for Kevin and his partners to respond before the deadline set out in Matterhorn's partnership agreement: the close of business two days later. Ralph intended to use the deadline to prevent Kevin from raising enough money to reverse the offer.

Years after the shotgun clause incited the fight for Matterhorn Cryptography, Kevin ran into Ralph's lawyer, Greg, who offered some insight into Ralph's business dealings. Likely sharing too much, Greg told Kevin that he had handled the majority of Ralph's business for the firm since the prior partner who brought Ralph on as a client had retired. It had only taken Greg a few months to understand the logic in

Ralph's approach but he also felt many of Ralph's tactics were distasteful. Ralph certainly always made sure what he did was legal and followed all contractual requirements. Ralph just wasn't the kind of client that Greg liked to bring up in discussion with other lawyers at his firm.

In a moment of humility Greg said that the shotgun clause had been Ralph's idea and that Greg had initially tried to debate it with him but quickly realized he would not be dissuaded.

Whenever he remembered that day, it made Kevin think of being buckled in tightly at the start of a roller coaster ride: hearing the slow clicking of gears as the cart is drawn slowly up the steep slope towards the inevitable adrenaline-saturated plunge, when the gears would be drowned out by passengers' screams as the track drops away from view.

*****

Even before he'd received the paperwork that triggered Ralph's shotgun, Kevin's day had begun with worrying news.

"Kevin."

"KEVIN!"

He heard it again, but this time it didn't sound like a voice in a dream. The voice had an anxious edge to it bordering on distress. A hand pushed his shoulder back and forth and he responded automatically by saying in a monotone, "What?"

"Something is wrong Kevin; are you awake?" Jenny said. Jennifer and Kevin had been married for 12 years at that point. They had two kids and believed they were on their way to a third. Jennifer had been ecstatic when she saw the little blue plus symbol on the pregnancy test stick seven weeks ago. Kevin had wanted a third, too, but shared more in Jennifer's happiness for the pregnancy than it being a source for his own.

Kevin had still been sleeping when Jenny woke up and started getting ready for the day. She had complained of a headache the night before. Now she was standing above Kevin in her pink bathrobe, shaking his shoulder to wake him.

"Did you hear me?" she said. "I'm bleeding."

"Huh, what is it?" Kevin mumbled, still blinking awake.

"I don't know. Are you listening? I saw some blood on the inside of my leg when I just went to get in the shower." The tension was visible around Jenny's eyes as she said it.

"Isn't that a normal thing to happen about now?" Kevin replied, finally coming around he tried to downplay any concern.

"No!" Jenny reacted, "it isn't normal at all."

Kevin then remembered Jenny having a miscarriage quickly after testing positive for her first pregnancy before getting pregnant again with Melissa. He knew miscarriage was more common on a first pregnancy but didn't think it was supposed to happen after having two healthy kids.

"Ok, I don't know, It's just — you are healthy and strong so it's probably fine," Kevin said, now starting to wonder too. "Do you want me to take you to the doctor's office to see what she says?", "Wait."

"What?" Jenny stared at him.

"Oh shit, I have that big meeting this morning that I was telling you about. This is the one where we'll hopefully close the big new contract," Kevin said, still trying to fit the pieces together. "How about we call to find out what time the doctor can see you, then figure it all out?"

"I am feeling fine to take myself, I can drive over to the doctor's office after the kids are at school."

"Are you sure?" he said.

"Yes, but keep your phone nearby just in case."

"Of course," he added quickly trying to make it sound like something he would've done anyway.

Jenny then called the number for booking priority appointments with her obstetrician and left a message. Kevin could see Jenny allow herself to take a deep breath. Her doctor was the best in the city and always responsive.

*****

Kevin left the house promptly. He wanted to get to the office early enough to review his company's financials with time to spare before the big pitch meeting scheduled for 10:30 am. The prospective client company, GPK Software, had a team coming over to Kevin's office but they all had to leave by noon. Kevin also had a lunch meeting booked with an old friend. His sales team felt strongly that he should be there for the presentation and final negotiations that day.

Kevin, being the CEO, was prepared to be in as many meetings as it took to land this new contract given it had the potential to increase Matterhorn Cryptography's revenue by 30%. Kevin had been pushing the sales team hard to close this new business because it would get them over the hurdle they had all been working towards for their bonuses. Two of the other executives, Simon Hunt and Sarah Bell, who Kevin had recruited in the beginning when they signed on their very first client, were close to reaching their targets that allowed them to buy into Matterhorn. Kevin liked working with Simon and Sarah and hoped they would stay with the company for many years to come. He was looking forward to giving them the good news himself.

Hopefully, the team from GPK would tell them their answer at the end of the meeting today. They had been courting this contract for over a year now and had heard confidentially from someone who worked for GPK that an internal deadline would force them to make a decision this week.

Kevin hated to rush out of the house leaving Jenny to organize the kids after her call to the doctor. He hoped everything was all right but his gut feeling was telling him otherwise. If he could just get this new client confirmed then he could rush back after lunch with some good news and deal with whatever came next.

Just before turning the corner out of the neighbourhood to get onto the highway his phone buzzed with a text message alert from Jenny. Kevin looked down quickly to see her message.

"You'll do great (kiss emoji). Will let you know what the doctor says. Appointment confirmed for 11:30 am," her text read.

"What an amazing woman," he thought. "She is stressed about her pregnancy and she's still thinking about my stuff."

He never did believe in the idea of love at first sight but when he thought back to the day he first saw her, he remembered being drawn to her immediately. Maybe that's what it feels like? He could vividly remember the way she looked that day. Her warm chestnut brown hair was tied back in a small ponytail that bounced weightlessly when she moved. Her features were precise. With her little button nose and angular jawline she reminded him of a fitness instructor for some reason. She had on a finely knitted ivory sweater that hugged her slim figure. Her small aquamarine earrings seemed to draw attention to her neckline and refined features. She was looking down at fruit in the boutique grocery store just off campus. That was one of only three times he had ever been in that store which made him think that seeing her that day could be his only chance to talk to her.

He still couldn't believe he had found the courage to walk up to her. After he fumbled out a few stilted sentences she agreed to meet for lunch the very next day. It was amazing how easy she was to talk to. They ended up struggling to find a way to end their conversation after two hours at the cafe. He learned many things about her that day including how she was studying to work in health care management. After that lunch date, the rest was history.

"Hey Siri" Kevin dictated,

"Send a text to Jenny saying, 'Thanks — I love you'." His phone properly transcribed it this time, surprisingly, and he confirmed to send it.

*****

Kevin walked out of the presentation meeting for GPK with a grin on his face. Everyone representing the GPK Software was positive and nodding along throughout the presentation. The vibe was great. They couldn't sign the initial services agreement in the meeting as they needed one other person's signature from the company but everything they said confirmed to him it was going ahead.

Kevin pulled out his phone to send a text to Jenny and see how she was doing.

"How's it going — are you done with the doctor?"

"Haven't seen her yet. She had to go to the hospital on short notice to deliver a baby this morning. I got pushed back to 12:45," Jenny responded after a minute. "I'm going to get something to eat at the cafe next to the clinic"

"Ok — hope you are feeling all right," Kevin added.

"Not great, getting cramps below my belly button," Jenny texted back.

"Crappy. Let me know as soon as you are done with the doctor. The meeting with the potential client went great. I know we are going to get the contract now. Love you."

Kevin finished and then waited a moment for another response but nothing came. Now he wasn't sure what to think. Both prior pregnancies had gone well without complication. He was looking forward to seeing his friend for lunch though and knew he and Jenny could handle whatever was to come, after all, they always had. Grabbing his sport coat from the closet and his keys from his drawer, he headed out for the restaurant to meet his friend Rob Wells for lunch.

*****

Driving up to the Fig Tree Bistro, one of his favourite restaurants in town, Kevin saw an unmistakable burgundy Audi parked in the lot. "It looks like Ralph Heinz is here for lunch too," he thought to himself. He had met Ralph a few years ago when they were first starting up their business. After a mutual friend's introduction, he had convinced Ralph to be one of their bigger early investors to fund the growth of the company. Ralph was known around town as an active venture investor.

Kevin remembered Ralph being surprisingly insightful about the strategies they planned on using to build the software business. They were one of the earlier companies to focus on cyber security as their main offering just before several high profile security breaches made headlines. The companies featured as victims in the media experienced such a drop in their share prices it forced businesses everywhere to scramble for ways to better protect themselves.

Kevin thought that he and Ralph would've spent more time together than they had over the years but he appreciated Ralph's willingness to back the business when it was a young start-up.

It had been a few months since he had seen his good friend Rob. He had known Rob since university and every couple of years they would plan an alpine climbing trip with two of their other friends. This year's adventure was coming up in a month. Kevin always looked forward to these mountain trips with excited anticipation. He even found himself daydreaming about the mountains for weeks in advance.

Walking into the restaurant he spotted Rob right away. The restaurant had an Italian themed interior with one large fig tree under a rectangular peaked skylight into the middle of the main seating area. The area where the majority of the tables were placed was two steps down from the front reception and the ceiling was more than a storey and a half up. The expanded interior height and second bank of windows that stretched up to the top of the front wall gave the restaurant a bright airy ambiance. There were "old world" Italian decorations on shelves and archetypical pictures hanging on the walls. There was one revealing painting of a woman hanging on the large back wall that was rumoured to be a likeness of the owner's wife when she was in her early twenties. That painting, along with some other provocative art pieces located in the hall towards the restrooms, seemed to infuse the restaurant with a charisma that attracted successful and influential people from all over the city.

As Kevin weaved his way through the tables and chairs he walked right past where Ralph was sitting almost without realizing it. When Kevin looked at Ralph, it was obvious that he hadn't shaven which wasn't unusual as most days Ralph had some stubble around his salt-and-pepper beard. He was wearing grey slacks and a light yellow collared shirt. His shirt didn't fit properly and had come untucked. As usual he had on three gold rings. The rings included his wedding band plus the ring from his alma mater on his left hand, and his favourite ring on his right hand, a larger gold ring with an inlayed square-cut low-profile opal stone. On each side of that ring, and only visible when he spread his fingers out, there was an outline of a scorpion.

"Oh, hello Ralph," he said. "It's a great day out there today isn't it?"

"We'll change that in a hurry won't we," Ralph said with an odd smile on his face and then continued. "What a surprise to see you here Kevin. I hope you are doing well," Ralph put his glass of JD on the rocks back down on the table. Ralph always had a controlled way of speaking. It didn't exactly seem warm and friendly even though the words he used were meant to be polite. Kevin then looked at the person Ralph was seated with and couldn't recall ever meeting her before.

The woman sitting across from Ralph had silvery blue eyes and an intensity to the way she stared back at Kevin. Ralph then added, "This is Lauren, I don't think you two have met. Lauren, this is Kevin. He is the CEO of Matterhorn Cryptography, the software company I invested into."

Lauren and Kevin broke the silence following Ralph's introduction by speaking at the same time.

"Nice to —" "Hi, how —"

"Ok, you first," Kevin attempted again.

Lauren then stood up to shake Kevin's hand and in doing so stepped quite close to him. The restaurant didn't have a lot of room to move around but it seemed as if her assertive stance was her default approach to people. Kevin straightened his neck and leaned his head back slightly as a natural reflex. She had an energetic handshake and clearly, this was not a casual lunch meeting between the two of them.

"Nice to meet you Kevin," Lauren said while handing him a business card. "I have a very good friend who works at GPK, the company you guys have been pitching. He said there was a big meeting today. I hope it went well for you?"

Kevin's eyes grew wider as he took in what she said. Lauren was having a magnetic effect on him. She was wearing a light taupe business skirt that did not look like it came off the rack. She had on a thin gold linked necklace and a similarly expensive looking gold watch

"Well, our team is the best out there right now," he said after a slight hesitation, trying to regain some ground without disclosing too much. Then after a pause that felt like Lauren was looking for him to say more, Kevin decided he didn't want to linger. "Ralph

— we should catch up soon. It could be good timing to have a call next week."

"Oh sure. I will be travelling starting Tuesday but let's connect on Monday if we haven't spoken by then." Kevin thought Ralph's response was measured somehow but immediately dismissed it. He looked over to see where Rob was waiting at their table and Kevin felt his stomach growl.

"It's a pleasure to meet you, Lauren, have a great lunch. The Fig Tree never disappoints," Kevin said as he started moving towards the table where Rob was seated. He took one last look at her business card with a raised eyebrow before putting it into his pocket.

"You too and best of luck," Lauren replied as she sat back down.

Ralph was looking at his phone as he gruffly said, "talk soon Kevin," and waved with his other hand. Ralph had just received an email notification.

As Kevin was walking away he could hear Ralph say to Lauren, "This should be a good week."

*****

Kevin texted his wife Jenny to check in just as the final bill came for lunch. He paid the tab and said goodbye to Rob. He hadn't seen a response back from Jenny by the time he was ready to leave the restaurant so he decided to head back to the office before calling her. Kevin was hoping there would be formal feedback from the sales team regarding the client's decision on the new contract and would have liked the news before heading over to meet Jenny.

It was always good seeing Rob, he thought. The conversation, his sense of humour and his positive outlook on life were all good reminders why it was always enjoyable to climb mountains with him. The weather over the mountain range they planned to go into this year had left a heavy snowpack which would take longer to melt out. Rob had made the point that he didn't mind more hard-packed snow in the gullies as it could be faster to hike up than loose rock. Their trip was still four weeks away which gave him plenty of time to finish collecting items from the list for supplies and extra gear he still needed. Rob, always being organized for these adventures, had emailed a checklist to Kevin and the other two guys who were going this year.

*****

Pulling into his parking spot outside the office Kevin sent another text to Jenny before getting out of the car. Starting to worry now he could feel a pit opening up in his stomach. She would have called him right away after seeing the doctor. He decided to call her while walking up to the front door of the office building. It was a warm sunny day but with the pressure of getting the new client signed on and Jenny's issue not being resolved yet, he was feeling increasingly tense.

His call went immediately to voicemail. "She must have turned her phone off," Kevin said aloud.

"What?" said Jessica — a woman who worked in the accounting group for the company who happened to be near the reception area as Kevin walked in. He was still looking down at his phone and looked up when she said it.

"Oh nothing, just trying to get hold of Jenny."

"This envelope here looks like it's for you," Jessica said as she happened to look down at the front desk to see a courier package with Kevin's name on a sticky note attached to it.

"Hmm, wasn't expecting anything today," Kevin said.

When he picked up the envelope and peeled off the note, he saw that it was from the law firm Ralph used. "That's strange, I just saw him at lunch," Kevin trailed off as he spoke and began walking towards his office while opening the envelope. Jessica didn't quite hear what he said but Kevin was already out of earshot walking the other way.

Kevin got the document out of the envelope and closed the door to his office. He started scanning the first page and saw the words "shotgun clause" halfway down. His heart started to beat out of his chest. Trying to focus, he began reading again from the top, going through all the details.

Then his phone started ringing. He let it ring two more times while still attempting to read more of the document he was holding. Finally tearing his eyes away, he saw Jenny's name on the screen and immediately swiped to accept the call.

"Hello, are you ok?" he said hurriedly.

"Kevin," he heard Jennifer say in a choked-up voice. "The doctor couldn't find any heartbeat." He could tell she was almost in tears. "I started getting bad cramps when I got into the examination room and then I realized that I was bleeding again."

"I don't understand," Kevin said. He was stunned. Now too numb to register any emotion for what he was hearing. His voice had gone flat in defence.

Jenny tried to explain more but was now audibly sobbing, "The doctor says that it's a miscarriage and the baby is lost."

"But, you are so healthy and have already had two successful pregnancies?" Kevin said.

"The doctor says there is always a risk of a chromosomal... something, which can cause a miscarriage. Now we have to decide if I am going to let it end itself naturally or go to the hospital for a procedure." Jenny was now just reciting what she heard as a way to control her tears.

"I am going to get in my car and come there right now," Kevin said with shortness of breath. "See you in 15 minutes."

"Ok, see you soon," Jenny said, choked up again.

*****

Shouting at Simon to say he was heading out for a bit as he jogged out the door to his car, Kevin couldn't decide what he would do when he saw her. Not allowing his mind to spin out of control, fear stopped him from beginning to accept these new circumstances. While driving to meet Jenny he tried to read the rest of the document that he still held in his hand. He would scan a few more lines every time he stopped at a red light. By the time he got to the doctor's office, he finally had an understanding of what it was.

Ralph intended to buy out his shares and had set the price he was going to pay. It said Kevin could buy Ralph out, but he would have to confirm that he had the funds to do it in less than three days — by the end of business Friday. To keep his stake in the company Kevin would need to come up with more money than he had or could borrow given the equity in their house. He was at a loss as to why Ralph was doing this. What did he think he could do without Kevin running the business? He started to think about getting the funds together but it was an overwhelming obstacle. He couldn't imagine selling the company right now, especially after all the work that had gone into building it up the last three years. Kevin's mind was racing. This was too much all at once.

*****

Walking up to the front of the clinic Kevin tried to take a deep breath to steady himself before going inside. Then he was led by a clinic staff person to the room where Jenny was waiting, and carefully opened the door.

Jenny was sitting in a soft chair looking at her phone when he came into the room.

"They finished the paperwork and gave me a prescription for some moderate pain killers. They said I could just wait in here until you arrived since I thought you were only going to be a few more minutes." Jenny was able to finish the sentence before tears started streaming down her cheeks. Kevin knelt beside the chair and leaned over to gently hug her. Not knowing what to do or say at that moment. The memory of holding each of their first two kids in his hands just after birth faded in and out of his mind. The pride of that moment and rush of emotions felt like a counterbalance to the pain he could see Jenny was experiencing.

Kevin tried telling Jenny about his memories of their children, Mella and Danny, being born and how appreciative he felt as a father for having healthy children. He could tell it had some effect and Jenny was able to catch her breath.

"I think I am going to get the procedure done at the hospital," Jenny said, adding a sense of finality to the pregnancy. "The procedure can be done in less than 10 minutes and I will be under anesthesia for it. It's the best way to make sure there aren't any complications."

"I'm sorry Jennifer," Kevin said as the acceptance that the baby was gone had sunk in. "Does it hurt right now?"

"Not as much as before. I had one pain killer when the doctor finished her diagnosis."

"When would you go to the hospital for the procedure?" Kevin asked.

"Tomorrow morning. I would be ready to come home after the kids have gone to school," Jenny replied.

They sat there looking down at the floor a little while. Then it felt like it was time to go.

"Do you want me to drive you home and then I can go and get the kids and come back and pick up my car later?" Kevin said.

"Yes, let's go. I want to lie down and rest," Jenny said with a defeated tone.

Taking Jenny home in her Range Rover kept Kevin from thinking about the documents he had received until he drove back out to pick up the kids from school. In a sudden jolt, the thought of what he had to do struck his mind like an electric shock. Kevin frantically got his lawyer on the phone to tell him about the notice he had received. He asked his lawyer to open up the company's shareholders' agreement and verify Ralph was allowed to trigger the shotgun clause and what the conditions were. Since he didn't have the documents with him (they were still sitting on the passenger seat of his car parked outside the clinic) he tried to recite what he remembered reading. He said he would send a copy of the document to his lawyer that night after he went back to pick up his car.

The conversation about his legal options left him feeling squeezed tighter than when he'd first read the notice. It was going to be an all-out sprint to raise the funding needed to keep an ownership stake in the company. "If we can land the new contract, then I can pay back whatever I have to borrow to match the shotgun offer," Kevin thought to himself. "I am going to have to meet with Simon and Sarah first thing in the morning to give them the news too. Holy shit. They aren't going to take this well. Simon just bought his first house." He continued to think through different sources of funding and options for raising the total. Kevin's thoughts bounced back and forth between worry for his team's reaction and resolve to fight back.

He had to keep hold of this company he built. He kept thinking, "I was actually looking forward to today. Lunch with Rob. The big pitch. What now with Jenny? She feels terrible and I don't know if we are going to keep trying. I assume she still wants to have a third but after what she is going through I don't know." He then stopped thinking and began yelling into oblivion, as if trying to argue with a future version of himself.

"What the fuck just happened," Kevin shouted while still driving. "What the fucking fuck!"

Chapter 2
TAKE OVER

Mellissa and Daniel didn't resist getting through the morning routine quickly. When Kevin woke them up and said that mommy was at the hospital and that he would have to pick her up after dropping them off at school, neither of them resisted getting out the door on time.

Kevin got them some breakfast and packed their lunches for school. Deciding what to put in Mellissa's lunch was like trying to solve a puzzle. Mellissa, or "Mella," as they all called her, was on the autism spectrum and had several peculiar personality traits. She was brilliant in many ways such as her comprehensive vocabulary which she had started developing at an early age. She was only nine years old, but talking to her was like speaking to an adult. Not only did she understand the meanings for a huge variety of words but she also had an uncanny perception for subtle sarcasm or irony. When it came to food, however, her palate had not evolved much from when she was a toddler. It seemed like the food Mella would eat had to be bland, simple or full of sugar. Kevin and Jenny worried about Mella's health, but most days it was a challenge to get her to eat anything so when she did it felt like more than just a pedestrian accomplishment.

Daniel, on the other hand, was always happy to feed. Mella's younger brother by just over two years was a growing all-around athlete and consequently was always starving. It seemed like 30 minutes wouldn't go by without hearing Daniel say, "I want food!" Kevin crammed everything into Danny's lunch kit and held the top down while cinching the zipper around, hoping it wouldn't burst from being overfilled. Their backpacks were finally ready.

"Mella, Danny, we are leaving in three minutes," he said. Mella seemed to transition out of the house more easily whenever she was given a set timeline.

After they all climbed into Jenny's dark navy Range Rover, Kevin paused a moment before pulling out of the driveway, mentally preparing himself for a challenging day.

Daniel took notice from the back seat. While Mella was usually oblivious to the body language of others, Danny, on the other hand, was an empath. He seemed to know immediately what someone else was feeling. He didn't always vocalize it but the expression on his face showed concern. Kevin mustered a smile, nodded to him in the rearview mirror, and then said, "Off we go."

Kevin got through traffic easily to arrive at the hospital 20 minutes before Jennifer was expected to be ready. He sat in his car looking at the front of the looming building. At any other time in the past when he had been there he wouldn't have paid much attention to the details of the facade. It would've been just another stop during a busy day. Today this place held his gaze. He wondered how many other fathers had been where he was sitting, staring at this building as if pleading for it to deliver their loved ones back to them healthy and unharmed. How many sons or daughters or other relatives would have come here over the years and sat just the same, reluctant to go in. People all wishing they didn't have to face what was real.

The central bulk of the hospital building was eight storeys tall with exterior walls that were clad in a beige brick. The lowest level was sunken down half a storey and was solid painted concrete that rose up to the top of the staircase leading into the main front doors. At some point in its history a new emergency ward building was added on the left end and was built at grade, presumably making it easier to get patients in on wheeled stretchers. There were slight vertical relief lines across the front where the wall stepped forward and backwards for every two stacks of rooms. Other than the small extended vestibule around the front doors and the vertical relief lines there were no other architectural features on the original portion of the hospital. It seemed to be missing an uplifting spirit that could provide hope to visiting families. Kevin knew the hospital was launching a major fundraising campaign to build new surgical suites, and wondered if it might be worthwhile to raise a little extra money to provide a more welcoming entrance.

While sitting in the car trying to push off the eventuality of going into the hospital, Kevin tried to take his mind off things for a moment while flipping through the day's newspaper. There was a front page article about the growth in the value of housing and how expensive homes in their city had become. He thought about how they had sold their rental house the prior year and wished they had held onto it. He wasn't able to focus well enough to read the articles so he threw the paper back down on the passenger seat with a slap and turned to stare out the window.

Kevin avoided entering the hospital whenever he was there to pick up Jenny during the normal work week. He could still remember that distinct smell of antiseptic hanging in the air. The pervasive clinical odour in the hospital made a hint of nausea ripple through his stomach just thinking about it.

Fortunately, Jenny's procedure at the hospital went as planned, with no complications. Kevin finally got out of the car and went in to find her just as she was walking back to the check-in area. Once they were in the car heading home, Jenny told Kevin about the experience. She described having a very different feeling going to the hospital that morning than when she had gone in to start her new job a decade prior. Her job after graduating from university started her out in the staffing management group with human resources at that very same hospital.

"When I went into the hospital for my first day of work I remember being excited about the new beginning to my life," she said. "This time when I walked through those same front doors, it was for the absence of a beginning."

Kevin reach over to rub her shoulder while glancing back and forth between her and the road. It was hard to find anything thoughtful to say at the that moment.

She was told by the nurses that her cramps were likely to continue for a few more days but the doctors said that the procedure was a success. It was hard to think of it as a success by any measure though. Given what they had lost Kevin didn't know how to start the conversation with Jenny to see if she still wanted to have another child. He figured he would let her bring it up when she was ready.

Kevin had been up late into the night writing emails and making a list of potential investors. He was anxious to get back to turning the table on the shotgun offer. When he started thinking about what Ralph was doing, bile began to rise in his throat. Kevin couldn't believe Ralph had this in the works while smiling at him in the restaurant yesterday.

"That conniving snake," Kevin said to himself after he had dropped Jenny off at home, now thinking of Ralph while driving to the office. Kevin planned to sit down at his desk, follow up last night's emails, and then prepare to meet his banker to see how much money he could borrow on short notice.

He had started to speed up in all of his actions. Kevin's metabolism felt like pushing a race car into the red zone, going faster and burning hotter than he could sustain for more than a day or two but he needed all the adrenaline his body would supply. He now had to narrow his focus onto only the critical tasks to reach his funding goal. Kevin delegated everything else to other executives for them to pick up the slack over the next two days while he did one thing: raise capital. He had met with Simon and Sarah an hour ago to tell them what was going on. Not surprisingly they were both unsettled by the news but what he didn't expect was for them to come forward and offer to personally fund as much as they could. He was blown away by the gesture and hoped it wouldn't come to him needing their funds. He also emailed several closer business contacts about the capital he needed to raise. There had been some leads but they all had lots of questions on the state of the company and its software services. Each new question took time that he did not have.

Now, the only thing that seemed to matter for the company was countering the shotgun. Nothing else was germane to him if he didn't hold onto an ownership stake. All of his other emails and daily to-dos melted away into irrelevance if he wasn't an owner anymore.

While Kevin was preoccupied with funding the shotgun clause, if he gave himself time to think, he was also worried about what either outcome would mean to the family. To succeed he would have to go into more debt. They already had a big enough mortgage payment given what it cost to build their dream home last year. If he wasn't able to complete the buyout he would receive some money for his shares but what would happen to his income? How long would they still be able to afford their car payments and mortgage payments unless another high-salary executive role came along right away?

"We'll be fine," he told himself optimistically. "We are going to land the new contract and the company will be worth more than Ralph is offering." His plan was to finance the buyout with debt and then pay off the debt with the additional income that would hopefully come in. Plus he would be a majority controlling shareholder so he could make the decision on what to do with the company's profits. Once Kevin owned a controlling stake in the company he could use cash from the company itself to proportionally pay out to all the shareholders. In effect he would be using the company's resources to take control of it.

Later in the day after back-and-forth emails and calls with potential investors Kevin had received responses from most of them saying they were not comfortable investing at this time. Kevin wondered if any of them had spoken to Ralph and if he had somehow convinced them to stay away. Many of the people he spoke with had known Ralph was his original investor because he had talked about it years ago when the company was a start up.

Now his only hope was to get financing from the bank. He started gathering up hard copies of all of the supporting information he had prepared for the bank including financial statements. He would need the bank to move faster than they normally liked to operate. He had known the commercial banker he was meeting with in the afternoon in a personal capacity for over 10 years but the banker would have to get his boss and credit manager to sign off on anything he did. That could take time.

Kevin felt a wave of uncertainty wash over him. On his way out of the office he couldn't think of any other possibility that would get him to the target. In that instant of desperation, the only safe passage his mind could latch onto was an absolute belief his bank would come through. If they didn't he would fail, but that was impossible.

*****

"As I had mentioned in my voicemail, we are up against a deadline to purchase more of the company and need to get financing approval as soon as possible." Kevin had been arguing about the company's financial strength with the three bankers for half an hour at that point and didn't seem to be making much headway. His friend Joe was one of the three and he was doing his best as the intermediary of the bunch but even Joe was running thin on patience.

"Look, Kevin," Joe started to build up momentum with his response. "Based on the process we need to go through to satisfy our lending criteria, which is always reviewed by our auditors, there is no way we can give you a binding commitment for a business loan on the amount you are asking for by tomorrow afternoon. The only kinds of loans we can commit to that quickly are secured real estate loans on residential property."

"So what you are saying is the company won't be able to get a loan but I could take out a bigger mortgage on my house?" Kevin felt like the conversation was a boxing match. He would jab or hook and they would parry or dodge and then jab right back.

"If you want us to look at what we can do for a new mortgage the best we could get you approved for in 24 hours would be 75% of your home's property tax assessed value. Because you are a long-standing client we would do that for you but it would have to be supported by a full appraisal which we would order to arrive next week. Usually, there is no issue with the appraised value but we have to disclose that condition to you if the buyout commitment you make tomorrow is contingent on our financing," Joe added.

"75% of tax assessed value?" Kevin repeated as a question to give himself some time to think, calculating in his head how much that would leave him short of the total amount needed.

"Yes, correct," Joe said.

"If that's all you can do then I guess I'll have to start with that." Kevin began thinking about what putting a new mortgage on the house would mean and resisted the idea because he knew it demanded a tough conversation with his wife. He didn't have time for the bank to hold back until he had spoken with her because by then they would be too late. They would have to get started working on the loan now, he would talk to her tonight and hopefully, she would agree. If she was against it then he would have to tell them tomorrow to put their pens down. He hated to do business like this but what other choice did he have if he wanted to meet the deadline?

"Let me know what information you need from me. Most of our home info should be in your files from when we did the loan last year after completing construction." Kevin felt like the roller coaster was well past the first highpoint in the track and with his nod for the bankers to proceed, it started accelerating downward at an uncontrollable speed.

"Yes, we should need very little new info from you. We will get started right away. Let's plan to talk before lunch tomorrow and we'll let you know where we stand" Joe could see by Kevin's body language he was ready to stand up and leave so he stood himself to extend his hand.

"Thanks, Joe, I appreciate your help with this," Kevin said while briskly shaking Joe's. He was being overly courteous with the bankers even if they were only able to provide part of the solution. After quickly saying the requisite goodbyes Kevin left the bank to head back to the office before going home. He would have to talk to Simon and Sarah, as much as he didn't want to. It might be necessary to take them up on their offer to come in for part of the funding in case the bank came in lower than expected. Even still, he would have to find at least one more investor to make up the difference because the new mortgage would never be enough. He was not looking forward to the conversation with Jenny that night.

"What a terrible time to have to even bring this up after what she's gone through in the last 24 hours," he thought while walking out of the bank.

Walking back into his company's office space was another reminder of why he needed to fight for the company. They had spent a long time with their architect before agreeing on the final version of the plans for their office space renovation. Kevin had read a story about the space that Steve Jobs had designed for the Pixar animation company's office. As an example, Jobs had taken extra time to select just the right brick colour for the exterior and created a unique centralized layout for the common space where staff would naturally congregate. The central traffic flow intersection created positive congestion that would draw people into collaborative situations. The attention placed on that office space design had inspired Kevin to put way more effort into carefully thinking through how their workspace should be laid out. They had modified every aspect of the space to open it up in some areas, reposition the layout in others, and created a style that was completely their own. There was no way he was going to let it all slip through his fingers tomorrow.

Kevin sent out several more emails before leaving the office to go home. Simon and Sarah instantly reaffirmed their support to join him in the buyout attempt. Kevin was inspired by their desire to keep the current management team together and that gave him a boost of energy to go out again to his investor contacts. He sent messages to some of the investors who had already said no, but this time his main point was that he and management were going to be committing over half the funds themselves. He thought this was a stronger position than when he was trying to get all funds from new partners so it was worth another shot with the same people.

When he was at home finishing up dinner that night all he could think about was the day that Jenny had just experienced. He was dreading what he would talk to her about next. Putting a new mortgage on their dream home was a very uncomfortable subject to bring up. They had spent so much time together planning the details for it and visiting the worksite while it was being built. Building it took lots of juggling. Before starting construction, they had to sell their rental property to cover the cost of purchasing the building lot. They also had to arrange construction financing to give them access to some of the equity in the house they were living in at the time before they sold it to move to the new home. Once their new home was built, however, it was all worth it. The family was so happy in the bigger home. The property it was built on had spectacular views of the city and was now very well landscaped. Jenny absolutely loved it. She had put her own touches on the design to personalize the spaces she cared about most. It was a great home and they all were truly happier in it as a family.

Now he was going to ask her to use the home to help fund a buyout at his company. "Matterhorn Cryptography was giving them the income that helped them qualify for the mortgage in the first place." He thought, which was just his way of rationalizing why it made sense to mortgage the home to keep control of the company and he simply couldn't think of another alternative.

"Jenny, a problem has come up at work." Kevin got her attention and set the stage. "There is something we need to discuss."

"Can it wait until the weekend? What is it?" Jenny said. She seemed drained of energy so her answer sounded like more of an obligatory response.

She was resting on the couch trying to watch a show while recovering from the trip to the hospital that morning.

"Sorry, no. Yesterday one of the main investors in the company gave us notice that he was exercising the shotgun clause in our agreement. Basically, it means that either I get bought out and no longer work at the company or I have to organize the funding to buy him out." Kevin tried to explain but wasn't sure if he was making any sense.

"What?" Jenny reluctantly said, not fully engaging in the conversation.

"The last two days have been crazy," Kevin added and didn't have to put any extra emphasis into his statement to show he was rattled.

"What are you going to do?" Jenny said.

"Last night I started emailing investors to see if anyone would come in. Today I met with Simon and Sarah who both surprised me by committing to fund all the money they could get access to. None of the investors were willing to commit so I went to the bank today to see what the company could borrow."

"What did they say?" Jenny's expression was defensive as if she was reserving her strength for something negative.

"Well, it's frustrating trying to get financing. The bank said they wouldn't be able to approve financing for the company by tomorrow. Joe said that all they could turn around on such short notice was a new home mortgage." The statement hung in the air with deafening silence.

"So you're asking can we refinance our house so you can put more money into the company?" Jenny said. Kevin could tell Jenny was thinking of what might happen.

"Yes, essentially," Kevin said in a reassuring tone, not all that convincing.

"I just don't know," Jenny said.

"I know we are going to land the new contract with GPK. This could be a great opportunity for us," Kevin said while trying to ignore his discomfort with what was going on.

"Fine, do whatever you have to do." Jenny sighed as she said it with a fatalistic tone.

"Ok, I will let you know how the day goes tomorrow. One way or another we will know by five o'clock." Kevin thought the conversation was easier than he'd expected. He couldn't help but wonder what else Jenny was thinking. Did she think this was his fault? Was she angry with him for even bringing up the idea? He couldn't see what other choice they had.

*****

It was almost lunchtime and the bank confirmed by email in the morning that they were making progress and would have an answer for him by 1:00 p.m. Joe had been Kevin's friend for a long time and had always worked hard to get Kevin's requests approved. But Kevin also knew Joe was constrained by the bank's hierarchy and sometimes he had been unable to get the necessary internal sign-offs. Kevin was still scrambling to get another investor on board. All of the replies he got to the emails he sent out yesterday were either a no or a not at this time. It was frustrating to be certain the company would be a great investment and still have people turn him down. At least Simon and Sarah were on board. They had borrowed some of their funds and even cashed in part of their retirement savings to back their buyout. Kevin wondered what

Ralph must be thinking. He probably believed Kevin wouldn't be able to come up with the money. He may not be wrong, Kevin thought.

When lunchtime came and went and still no answer Kevin started to imagine what it would be like to no longer work at Matterhorn. It was hard to visualize what he would do if he wasn't working there. It was simply unimaginable. He just could not believe that he wouldn't get the funding needed for the buyout.

At 1:18 p.m., an email showed up from Joe. Kevin immediately pulled it up and read it. It was good news. Joe confirmed that the bank was ready to provide a new mortgage on Kevin's home and they would go up to 80% of the tax assessed value. The reason for the increase is that property values had gone up in the last year and they felt comfortable with the higher amount. It was a conditional commitment and Kevin would have to get a new appraisal to substantiate the value. Kevin called Joe immediately to get more background and make sure he could trust the commitment. He needed to be certain the funds were going to be there even if Joe couldn't put it unconditionally in writing.

"The financing is approved!" Kevin said loudly as he walked into Simon's office. Sarah was standing next to Simon's desk so he delivered the news to both of them at once. Simon had gained a fair amount of weight over the last three years and as a result Sarah always seemed to be the one to visit him in his office. Sarah and Simon both let smiles break across their faces but Kevin's lips were pressed together tightly with determination.

"The bank surprised me and committed to more than I expected. But with the loan and the additional funds the three of us have available we are still only just over halfway to the amount we need,"

Kevin summarized. "And none of the responses from the investors have been positive."

"Wow. What now?" Sarah said. She had been holding her breath and finally let it out, unintentionally sounding deflated.

"I am going to call everyone that I haven't heard back from or didn't get a completely definitive no from," Kevin said as he straightened up in a defiant posture. Knowing he didn't have much time left he nodded to them and headed back to his office, squeezing his leg muscles as he walked making his footsteps land harder on the floor. He was going to get this done. He had to push. People needed to see the opportunity he knew was there.

*****

With each call he made his tone started sounding more and more strained. By the time he got a hold of the eighth potential investor, he was no longer wasting time on the phone with small talk. His pitch was simple, they had doubled in size the last two years and were on track to grow by at least another 25% this year. They had huge potential and the three key executives were putting up more than half of the buyout funds themselves. They needed another partner to fund the remaining amount. After quickly updating the investor on the financial position of the company and the details of the services they offered he would simply and boldly ask them if they could come in for the rest. The response on this eighth call was different. Kevin quickly realized there was an opening. It wasn't a straight-out no.

"What would it take for you to invest with us?" Kevin asked the investor.

"I don't know" came the reply, but it felt more like a negotiation than ambivalence. "I don't like the share price." The investor pulled back.

"The share price is set by the terms of the buyout. We can't change it," Kevin said, feeling stuck and not sure what else to do.

"Well, it's just too high, based on what you've said, and I don't believe you will continue to grow the business that fast next year. I would come in but the price would have to be lower," the investor countered.

"I don't know how we could do that," Kevin said, squeezing his temples with the thumb and forefingers of his left hand while trying to think of a solution. "The only way that would work is if we collectively fund the total amount but the three executives give you some of the shares that would have gone to us. Then you would get the price you want but it would mean that the management team and I would be paying more for our shares."

"That's up to you if you want to do it that way," the investor replied.

"Let me talk with the team and I will call you right back," Kevin said, giving himself a moment to think and an out.

After hanging up and leaning back in his chair with his head throbbing, Kevin decided it was worth it. The share price had been set by Ralph and with any luck, they would finalize the new contract with GPK soon which would make this all seem like a brilliant move by Kevin.

He discussed it with Simon and Sarah and they agreed. He called the investor back to confirm the details.

It was done.

The total amount of funding needed to counter the shotgun offer was ready and he could now get the lawyers to finish the formalities of wrapping up the transaction over the next two weeks.

On his way to the lawyer's office 10 minutes later to confirm the final version of the documents, he got a call from Simon.

"We just got emailed the signed contract from GPK!" Simon sounded ecstatic. He had probably put in the most effort of anyone on the details of that deal.

"You're kidding!" Kevin said back, nearly shouting into the phone with a huge smile on his face. "Ah, that is just great," he repeated, revelling in the moment.

"Thought you should know right away. Thanks for allowing us to become owners with you. We appreciate it," Simon said.

"Hey, you deserve it," Kevin said, feeling just as appreciative of what they had done together. "I will call you when we are done at the lawyer's office. You deserve to celebrate tonight. I won't be able to join you but take anyone out on the team you like for some food and drinks on the company." Kevin was thinking about Jenny and wanting to make sure he was there so she didn't have to worry about the kids while she was still getting her strength back.

*****

In Kevin's mind, he imagined what was going on at Ralph's office at that moment. He pictured Ralph screaming "What?!" At his lawyer on the phone and then hearing is lawyer trying to rationalize what had happened.

He imagined Greg explaining to Ralph that Matterhorn's lawyer had just confirmed that they were countering the shotgun and had the funding to buy him out. Then Greg would clarify that the notification had been received before the deadline, and they were ready to close within 14 days as the shareholders' agreement required.

Ralph would likely have been surprised. Kevin was sure that Ralph believed he would never have been able to come up with the money. Kevin knew Ralph liked his whiskey so being that it was late in the day on a Friday he was probably already four drinks deep into his usual, JD on the rocks. He seemed to always have a bottle around at the office whenever Kevin had been there meeting with him in the past.

Looking back on this moment years later, Kevin could see with hindsight that he had been celebrating too soon. Ralph always thought three steps ahead and what would happen next was all according to the plan that Ralph had laid out ahead of time with his other business relationships. While Kevin felt at the time that he had overcome the shotgun clause in the shareholders agreement, there were some very specific clauses that Ralph had purposefully excluded from the shareholders agreement originally, to his own benefit.

*****

Kevin was walking tall when he got home. Rob had called to confirm some of the details about their mountain trip while Kevin was making dinner for Jenny and the kids. He couldn't talk long but Rob commented that he sounded especially upbeat even for a Friday afternoon.

"What can I say, it was a full week," Kevin gregariously replied to Rob.

Finishing the call off and getting back to the family, Kevin was reminded of how good it would feel to have the new contract underway with GPK, have the share buyout closed, and get out with his friends for the alpine adventure at the end of the month.

Dinner was going to be casual tonight as Jenny was still not feeling great. The kids ate at the island in the kitchen sitting on stools next to Kevin. Jenny ate a small portion while propped up with some pillows on the couch. Kevin wolfed down his food quickly and left Mella and Danny in the kitchen to finish their meal. Mella was a very slow eater and he wanted to give Jenny a full update.

Kevin had texted Jenny before leaving the lawyer's office earlier to let her know they had gotten the full funding committed and won the big new client contract. He knew though that they still had to discuss the next steps to register the larger mortgage against the house.

"How are you feeling tonight?" Kevin said softly as he sat down on the couch near Jenny.

"My stomach is better now. The pain killers have helped," Jenny calmly responded.

"The bank confirmed they would provide us with the mortgage and one of the last investors on the list decided to come in to complete the funding. We got it done in time," Kevin said, sounding excited. But he didn't get the response from Jenny he was expecting.

"What do we have to do for the mortgage?" She asked.

"We will have to go in next week and sign some papers at the lawyer's office. They are going to have an appraiser come by on Monday to confirm its value.

They think the market is up so we probably have more equity in the home than we thought," Kevin said, again thinking it was more good news.

"All right, I hope it all works out," Jenny said, trying to be positive but her withered response made it sound like an omen. Kevin was also thinking about the bigger mortgage payment they now had and the fact that this was their family home and not the domain of the company. The home was in her and his name but he wasn't sure she was comfortable with the idea of signing her name on a loan that would go to something she had no involvement with.

Kevin could see Jenny was fighting the pain she felt from losing the baby. But he was so happy with the result of the business for the week he didn't have any real worries. Home values were up and the business was growing. He was feeling confident and didn't foresee any problem he couldn't handle. He wasn't sure when she was going to be ready to talk about babies again and still thought it better to wait for her to bring it up first. He got up to head back to the kitchen to clean up and then felt his phone vibrate.

When he fished his phone out of his pocket he saw a notification for a message from Lauren. She wanted to know if he could meet for lunch on a day the following week.

"Hmm," Kevin audibly reacted to seeing the message.

"What is it?" Jenny said as he was walking out of the room staring at his phone.

"Oh, nothing. Just normal work stuff," he said defensively, sloughing off the question, and then walked back to the kitchen.

Chapter 3
ROCK SLIDE

"It looks like the weather could be great next weekend," Kevin said to Rob. He was checking the mountain forecast on his phone while they were walking through the outdoor equipment store. They decided to meet a week and a half before the trip to purchase any remaining items on their list. Their other two friends Gerry (Gerrard) Hamilton and Doug Olson also met them at the store to get what they needed, too.

It had been raining hard recently but the skies were forecasted to clear with higher temperatures the following the week when they were scheduled to go on their climb.

Just as Kevin made his comment about the weather he looked over to see someone he thought he recognized.

"Hello Kevin," the woman looked up and said. She was browsing through some running clothing on a rack nearby.

"Oh, hi," Kevin said automatically, taking a moment to place where he knew her from. Then the memory from the Fig Tree Bistro hit him and he quickly added, "How are you, Lauren?"

Kevin was looking at her so he didn't notice the looks on the other guys' faces. Doug turned so that his back was to Kevin and winked and Rob and Gerry. They immediately knew what he was thinking. They all thought Lauren was stunning. She was athletic and had piercing blue eyes and long straight hair. Her appearance showed she paid attention to her looks but it wasn't obvious she was wearing lots of makeup.

"Sounds like you guys landed that contract. I hope the company is doing well?" Lauren said clearly but casually.

"Yes, thanks." Kevin started to think back to when he saw her at the restaurant and remembered that she was having lunch with Ralph while the shotgun clause notice was on its way to his office. He didn't know if she was aware of what had happened and her body language didn't belie that she was keeping any secrets. "I hope all is well with you. Have you seen Ralph since your lunch that day?" he said nonchalantly, trying to probe without hinting at his intention.

"No, I haven't; he's a busy guy," Lauren replied.

"Oh, well, our management team bought out his shares of Matterhorn Cryptography and I haven't talked to him since either," Kevin said, making it sound like it was a friendly mutual business transaction.

"Good for you. Sounds like you built some helpful relationships. It was good timing then?" She gave him a controlled smile.

"Everything is going well. Oh, that reminds me. I got your email regarding a meeting but was so caught up in the closing for the buyout I forgot to respond. Early next week on the Tuesday or Wednesday could work." Kevin wasn't certain that she was ignorant to Ralph's use of the shotgun clause, but her poise made him uncomfortable.

"Yes, Wednesday can work. I will send you an email to confirm," she replied. "Looks like you guys are

planning on going for a hike?" She added with a slight
smirk, guessing their plans by the freeze-dried food
packages they were picking out.

"Yes — we have a big trip coming up." He
didn't want to take any more time away from his friends
and finished with, "Ok, catch up next week."

He gave her a final nod, trying to retain his
composure and then tore his gaze away. His friends
chuckled. At least they were already having a good time
and the trip hadn't even started yet.

*****

Kevin was already second guessing agreeing to
meet Lauren for lunch before she even walked into the
sushi restaurant. He had arrived first and was initially
brought by the host to a table near the window but
asked for another alternative. Eventually being led
towards the back of the row of booths he decided to
sit down at a more inconspicuous table.

Lauren had selected the restaurant and Kevin
was unsure of why she wanted to meet but found it
hard to deny the invitation when she was standing there
in person the prior week. Every time he heard the door
open up as the lunch hour was beginning, his gaze
would twitch up towards the entrance, happening
dozens of times before Lauren was the one finally
walking in.

He saw the host quickly raise a hand to wave her
over to his location. She turned immediately to come
over while ignoring the last of what the host was trying
to say to her.

"I was rushing to get here, the traffic was
horrendous on the way over," Lauren was speaking
before she had made it all the way over to the table to

sit down. Briskly getting settled in the booth she wasted no time looking at the menu and calling the waiter over to order. Then, just as quickly, she dispatched the waiter before peppering Kevin with a string of questions that evolved from small talk into a pointed inquisition about the evolution of the security software industry.

Kevin was leaning back in his seat with his arms crossed while answering her, shortening the length of his reply with each successive question.

Eventually she eased off and asked him, "How is your family Kevin?" The subtle way she probed was like a nudge to someone walking carefully on a tightrope. Kevin was momentarily off balance and hesitated in his response.

"The family is great, everyone's doing really, really well." Kevin heard the sound of over-compensation in his own voice.

"That's great. From what I hear your business is growing handsomely." Lauren tilted her head slightly as she said it and gave Kevin a coquettish look.

"The team has worked especially hard over the last three years and it is all coming together," he countered, trying to keep the conversation on familiar ground.

Lauren stared at Kevin for a moment, not saying anything.

Kevin was at a loss though, searching for confirmation of what she was hinting at while continuing to maintain eye contact.

The next moment the waiter walked up with their food and broke the silence. Kevin's chest relaxed forward as he released his crossed arms and put his elbows down the table, ready to accept the meal.

"Thank you — this looks wonderful," Lauren acknowledged the waiter in a dismissive way. Turning back to Kevin she changed gears completely. "Do you follow the real estate market?"

"Not lately," Kevin shifted in his seat trying to get comfortable again. "I watched home values more closely when I had rental properties but since we moved into our new home and I sold off the last rental I haven't had much time to pay attention to it."

"Ah, well you are far better off than I am. I can't seem to find a decent home that's in my price range," Lauren replied.

"Oh yeah?" He murmured looking up from his meal with raised eyebrows.

"My brother bought a home years ago but I stayed out of the market thinking the prices would come off if I timed it right. In hindsight I shouldn't have waited. Now I am stuck out of the market."

"We all make trade offs for what's most important in our lives. I never had any issues buying real estate. Actually, the first property that I purchased was a rental, and ever since I continued to roll the equity along from one to the next," Kevin said. "I've never really understood the difficultly people have buying. Maybe I always just saw it as a fear to get over."

"I didn't see you as one to be condescending," Lauren countered with a sly grin.

"Oh, I didn't mean it like that," he stammered.

"I get it, I should live below my means and save more. Sure. You're right. Anyway, I'll figure it out eventually." She sat up straight against the back of the seat as she said it, staring at Kevin again with a sparkling intensity.

"What's next for you Kevin?" She said, clearly thinking about something while waiting for a response.

"This is the weekend I am headed out with the guys for our mountaineering trip. We are going up to climb Forsaken Peak. I can't wait to get out there." Kevin seemed to miss the direction of the question. He might not have missed it completely but was more excited about the alpine adventure than talking more about business.

"Oh, right. I hope it gocs well you," Lauren said.

The waiter appeared and lowered a dish with two mint candies and the cheque on it. Kevin grabbed the bill and put his credit card on top before either of them were able to fight over who would pay the tab.

"Thank you for lunch Kevin."

"Don't mention it. If you're putting in a good word for us helped us win the GPK contract then I should buy several lunches."

"Deal." Her wit caught him off guard.

"I meant, thank you," Kevin clarified sheepishly.

"Of course. If you don't mind, I am going to the use the ladies room before the waiter comes back."

"You know I actually have to run to get back to the office. Have a good rest of the day though." He reached out to shake her hand formally before turning to go.

Lauren's mouth was open as if she was going to say something else in response but then closed her lips before finally wishing Kevin off by shaking his hand and then said, "You too Kevin. Have a great afternoon. Best of luck."

"Thanks again," he said as he turned to go, briefly giving her a slight wave before walking out. Kevin was wondering what her intentions were with their conversation.

"Why did she even invite me to lunch?" Kevin thought to himself, deciding that he may have missed something.

*****

There was water flowing everywhere while the group of four was hiking through the forest on the way to the campsite for the night. They started the drive early Friday morning and it took the better part of six hours to get to the trailhead on the edge of the park. When they reached the end of the paved road where it narrowed and hugged the edge of the river heading upstream, they saw how much rain had come down the day before. The weather system had clung to the mountains a little longer than in the city and it was just starting to clear that afternoon. There were many places where the trail itself was flowing with water and two creeks that weren't usually there were flowing straight over their intended path. These shallow creeks were wide enough that they couldn't jump across so they had to wade through and then endure hiking with wet socks and shoes.

The sun was starting to peek through the clouds as it was setting. Occasionally on a bend in the trail that put them out above the main riverbed where there was a gap in the trees, the view of the mountains ahead would get them excited. Each time they caught a glimpse of a rocky peak their pace would accelerate for a time. The further they progressed the warmer it got so it wasn't too uncomfortable moving with wet feet.

With four hours of fully loaded hiking they had made it most of the way to base camp. Throughout the drive and the hike, they had all updated each other about everything that occurred in their lives since the previous mountain adventure. Kevin's description of recent events, with Jenny's miscarriage and the shotgun buyout along with his struggle holding onto the company, was the most riveting. His pride for growing his company was evident, but he was sounding unabashedly confident — talking louder, telling more obnoxious jokes, and expending energy in unnecessary ways. It was as if he felt his business success made him capable of handling anyone setting up a roadblock in front of him.

Rob and Kevin had the most climbing experience of the four. Rob had gone on several guided climbs and had always been a keen student of the guides, looking to pick up as many tips as possible about the right use of knots and the latest best practices with new types of gear. With Rob's technical knowledge he tended to be the de facto leader on these trips, also keeping close track of the route. On this trip there was a bit more tension in the journey. Without realizing it, Kevin's role as CEO was starting to become the persona he defaulted to most in other areas of his life. He was now generally more directive and decisive with people. They found this would mean giving less time for everyone else to provide their input or opinion if for Kevin it meant saving 10 minutes of discussion. The recent success he had experienced at work added to his self-image. He believed he was meant for a leadership role. Leadership wasn't something Kevin had studied or been given feedback on. His belief in leading at work was based simply on what resulted in more revenue and additional objectives being achieved.

*****

"We made it," Rob said after dropping his backpack to the ground in the middle of the flat spot where he planned to set up the tents. The rest of them let their shoulder straps slide off as they too lowered their backpacks to the ground.

"It's going to be an early morning." Kevin then added, "As always — an alpine start gets us on the route before the sun comes up." This meant setting alarms to wake up at 3:15 a.m. After consuming breakfast and confirming they had all the gear they would need, they planned to start heading up the base of the mountain by 4:15 a.m. They would be travelling lighter for their summit day tomorrow as they would leave most of their clothing, cooking, and overnight gear behind in the tents. Using their summit packs they would take only what was needed to reach their destination at the top of the mountain and then get back down before sunset.

*****

After a restless sleep and a quick breakfast of poorly cooked oatmeal and some fresh blueberries, the group of four set out to begin the climb. After 45 minutes of steep hiking up through the sparsely treed hillside, the sunlight started cresting the top of the ridge to the east. It was still earlier than Kevin normally would go for a morning workout so he could feel his sluggish metabolism straining to catch up. Waking and getting up the mountain early always left his stomach in a knot until about 6:00 a.m.

After coming out of the trees where the visible trail ended the next section of the climb would take them over scree to the base of the steeper rock. The loose rock scree slope was a mixture of baseball to basketball-sized rocks or larger that were only held in place because they settled on each other at the maximum possible angle before they would begin tumbling farther down. After slowly and carefully picking their way up through the rock scree, they got to the bottom of the slabs. The slabs were smoother flatter rock ramps that steepened as they rose towards the summit. "That sucked," Rob said as he traversed the final section of scree and finally found solid footing on bedrock. "Getting up scree is always my least favourite part of these trips." It was tedious when every step taken caused some amount of rock to tumble away. Not only did it take extra effort to balance, but the instability of hiking on scree took unceasing concentration which wore on the nerves. As they all came together at the top of the scree slope, the rock became more solid but there were wet mossy areas to watch out for in several spots. They had to constantly adjust their route to stay on dry rock as they travelled diagonally upward and over the slabs.

After 15 minutes of moving up the medium angle slope, they were fast approaching the bottom of the steeper gullies where the real climbing would begin. There was a small row of sketchy rock that began sliding out as Doug started to step on it. The rocks quickly skittered out under his feet, sending him down towards Kevin on his side, tearing part of his nylon pants and scraping the side of his leg. "Ah, shit!" he shouted but was able to instantly arrest his slide. Doug's body was quivering when his feet stopped sliding. All of his knuckles where white and as his hands clung to surface of the rock, he repositioned his feet to get comfortable. He kept his face close to the rock for a moment, hiding his expression from the view of the other guys. They had been comfortable without ropes up to this point because it wasn't steep enough to fall but with loose rock, a slide was certainly a risk.

Kevin sidestepped the last of the small rocks rolling towards him and then decided to get in front of Doug so he could be the one checking for stability in the route.

"Hey Doug, are you good?" Kevin inspected Doug's leg as he drew near. He bent to take a closer look at where the rip was to check if there was any blood.

"Yeah, just a scrape. It stings and will probably bruise but nothing major," Doug said, still lying with his chest now on the rock.

"You want to hang back a sec and I will get out in front?" Kevin asked while Doug was catching his breath.

"Sure. You go first now," Doug confirmed.

After double-checking to make sure Doug wasn't hurt, Kevin stepped around him and continued to advance their position. Within a minute of being out in front, he came to a point where he had to stretch his leg over a strip of rock that was dark with water still trickling out of the saddle between the mountain and the adjoining ridge. He stepped over the dark patch onto a particularly smooth spot of basaltic granite. Not realizing there was still moisture on his boot from where he had passed by Doug, as he took the weight off his back foot to step higher, his front foot slipped out before he could get his other leg up in front of him.

Kevin slammed down right onto the wet mossy band covered with a thin film of water and hammered his shoulder into the unforgiving rock. Unable to get a hand on a dry hold to steady himself, he started sliding down towards the scree slope.

It all happened so fast he couldn't even react. It was like looking out at the world from the eyes of a child stuck on a carousel that had been spun exuberantly by an adult. As he tumbled, his cheek smacked violently against the rock. Even though his helmet was protecting his skull he managed to hit the rock at just the wrong angle. He had just received the knockout strike of a mixed martial arts fight. His body was paralyzed for a moment, continuing his slide down, all he could do was take in the hazy distorted sights and sounds he was experiencing. It was like being in a dream without having motor control of his arms and legs.

The slope where Kevin started to slide wasn't that steep so he didn't pick up tremendous speed as one would in near free-fall. The wet rock was not perfectly smooth so there was some friction to keep his stiff body from falling too fast.

The other three guys were too far away to get a hand on him and slow his descent. Rob was first yelling at Kevin and then at the other guys hysterically. They were dumbfounded and gripped by paralysis with what they were witnessing, watching their friend in terror as he careened away down the rock slope.

Kevin was still aware that he was seeing images with his eyes but was not able to think about what the images meant. He rolled through a few more rotations with visions of rocks spinning past his face. With one more stunning hit to his helmet, the blurry well lit images faded away, and he lost all understanding of time passing by.

*****

Eleven days later the doctors would stop the stream of chemicals in his IV that was keeping him in a medically induced coma. A test for brain activity had shown that medication was no longer necessary.

The top neurosurgeons who had been studying Kevin's condition had come to an agreement that the swelling was under control and it was time to see if Kevin would wake up. Brain condition aside, he escaped the accident with relatively few serious physical injuries. His internal organs were fine but one leg was broken just above the knee, one arm was broken halfway between the wrist and the elbow, and two vertebrae were cracked near the insertion points at the bottom of the rib cage. Jenny had been there daily, some days with the kids and some days on her own, but she could only stay long enough to hear him breathing and talk to the nurses on how he was doing. It caused an emotional tug-of-war for her, the longer she stayed in his hospital room, the more fearful for the future she became. Rob had been to the hospital more than anyone else to spend time with Kevin while he was unconscious. Rob felt personally responsible for what happened. He was supposed to be the one looking after their use of gear to make sure they were all safe. Even though he and Kevin had a similar level of climbing experience, he had spent enough time studying mountain guides' techniques and knew there was no reason to take risks during a mountain climb. There was always a safer way.

*****

The morning after Kevin was taken off the medication that had been keeping him out, he came to for the first time. Kevin woke up with bad indigestion, it was like he had sharp rocks in his belly that caused spasms in his stomach muscles, and his mouth tasted stale. He was still foggy and was speaking slowly, taking twice as long to come up with a simple answer to a question. The nurse brought in the two doctors who had been monitoring him and one of them filled Kevin in on what his treatment had included. He understood that he had fallen while climbing and was brought to the hospital. The doctor explained that he had suffered significant head trauma. He said that Kevin's brain activity was strong but they were worried that any swelling could cause long term damage so they decided to put him into an induced coma.

Once he was awake, more tests and verbal checks on his memory indicated there didn't seem to be any lingering effects on his cognitive function. He would still have to stay in traction for another week while the rest of his body was continuing to heal. He tried to describe the nightmares he vaguely remembered having. The doctors told him they had heard of cases where people experienced nightmares while in a coma but couldn't imagine what that would have been like.

Rob arrived for his daily visit a few hours after he came out of the coma. Rob came into the hospital room and slowly approached Kevin's bed to sit down near him. The skin on Rob's face went taut as it shifted through a mixture of expressions.

"Man, it is so good to see you with your eyes open. You scared the hell out of me. All of us," Rob said quietly.

"All I think of are the nightmares I was having while asleep," Kevin said, struggling to remember what happened when they were climbing. Kevin described his vivid nightmares to Rob. He had dreams about animals chasing him in the forest and also, strangely, about his software company's building crumbling down in an earthquake, trapping the staff in the rubble.

Rob began telling him what happened after he fell. "You tumbled a long way down before finally coming to a stop against a small juniper tree. We all started moving as fast as we could. When we got down to you, we thought you were dead." Rob had tears forming in the corners of his eyes when he got to that last word. "You were unconscious but breathing. It looked like the helmet took the brunt of the impact but it was cracked and the styrofoam padding was compressed in two spots where your skull must have bounced off the inside of it."

Rob continued. "You remember those two GPS locator beacons we brought? I pulled out the one in my pack, extended the antenna and turned in on as fast as I could. We knew we had to move you but were afraid we would do more damage. We used the hiking poles and ice axes to strap to your body and make it possible to carry you down. It took us over an hour to get you back down to where the tents were. Doug has some first aid training so he and Gerry stayed next to you while I stripped off all my extra gear and started running with my phone, car keys and water bottle back towards the parking lot." Rob's heart rate was racing again while telling the story, reliving the experience all over again. "I thought if I could call the ranger's office when I got a cell signal partway down the trail then we could get some help. It turned out there was a ranger already coming up to respond to the locator beacon signal. I was able to reach the emergency line for the ranger station and they confirmed they would send in a helicopter to get you out. I ran further down the trail

and met up with the ranger about two-thirds of the
way to the parking lot. We turned around and got back
to you just before the helicopter arrived. The ranger
had his satellite phone and was able to stay in contact
with the dispatch all the way up to our tents. The
helicopter crew had already been on standby after the
beacon signal report came in so they were able to get to
you relatively quickly once airborne."

"After all of the running, Doug and Gerry said I
should jump in the helicopter and ride back with you to
the hospital. They packed out the gear and drove the
vehicle back." Rob finished relating the events of
Kevin's extraction and started to breathe normally
again.

"You were at the hospital in just under six hours
after the fall. The ranger service was incredible and the
helicopter was able to fly you directly to the landing
pad at the hospital. I was terrified you were never going
to come back. I haven't ever had to watch anyone so
closely with their eyes closed during the day like that.
As the hours went by I kept thinking I should've been
the one in front." Rob could see that Kevin was still
needing to rest and heal. A moment passed as Rob was
watching Kevin's eye blink open and closed more
slowly. Then Kevin drifted off to sleep naturally, this
time without the nightmares.

When Kevin woke up again Jenny left home
quickly to see him. She heard Rob had been there just
after Kevin became conscious for the first time. The
hospital had notified her when Kevin had woken up
again late in the day. Kevin was already asleep again
though when she arrived. She was thankful to hear
from the nurse that he had been lucid and had spoken
with Rob. Seeing him sleeping with his eyes closed

made it seem like he was still trapped in a coma. She walked out without a cathartic release.

Jenny had left Kevin's phone at the hospital that night so he could text her when he woke up. She hoped the nurse on duty would show him it was there. Kevin finally sent Jenny a text when he found the phone the following morning and she texted back to say she was on her way. Dropping the kids off at school gave her more time to spend with Kevin without worrying about Mella or Danny. She didn't know how she was going to react to seeing him with his eyes open again.

Without noticing, Jenny was taking small steps as she entered his hospital room. As she came around the corner she could see Kevin looking up at the nurse and she paused for a moment and hesitated, not able to move.

The nurse looked up to see Jenny and said: "I will leave you two to catch up. He still has some healing to do. Make sure he doesn't try to sit up." The nurse saw the statement had registered with Jenny even though Jenny didn't respond so the nurse left the two of them alone.

Breaking through her momentary paralysis, she rushed to the side of the bed and leaned over to gently put her arm on his shoulder and pressed her cheek against his. Like a dam bursting from pressure on a crack, she started quietly but quite uncontrollably weeping into the pillow. He reached up with his good arm and squeezed the middle of her back. She wouldn't have heard it but he was breathing shallowly and tears had squeezed out of his tightly closed eyelids. They didn't say anything for a few minutes.

In that moment, memories of some of their shared experiences flashed back into his mind. First was one from the initial months after they had met. He was sitting next to her on a spot above the water line on a pebbled beach shore by the ocean in the summer. It was a memory that stood out in his mind because of how she had repeatedly reminded him of it over the years. Jenny had said it was one of her favourite memories of him from when they were dating. It was from his younger days when he was thin and tanned. He overheard her describing it to her friend once, saying his dark brown hair was cut short on the sides with two waves from the top pushed back towards his ears from a part that was slightly off centre. He was wearing classic style black Ray Ban sunglasses, a running watch, and a navy striped short sleeve collared tee shirt. The warm bright midday sunlight bathed the rocky beach and the trees beyond with an orange-yellow radiance. They ate lunch and enjoyed each other's company for hours.

The next image that came to his mind was of the time when they were seated on a bench beside a small pond in the gardens of the countryside inn where they had their wedding. Wanting to check on the place two weeks prior to their big day, they decided to stay a little while longer. After sitting down for dinner to test the food, they went for a walk as the sun was setting. It was just the two of them there watching the colour change in the sky as the afternoon turned into twilight. They talked about the details of their wedding, the people they would see, and ideas they had for starting a family in the future. It was another one of their perfect memories that she told him she wished she could relive again.

As the tension dissipated they both were able to take a full breath.

"It felt like being crushed, Kevin. Every day that I woke up not knowing if you were going to live or die was like having a stack of bricks piled up on my chest. These last twelve days have been the worst. I can't remember any other time in my life that has been like the last month and a half," she said.

"I don't know why all this happened. Everything was working for us," Kevin added simply, not able to think clearly enough to answer with deep thought.

The conversation followed that one-sided pattern for a while. Kevin was listening to what Jenny was saying but couldn't respond in a meaningful way. Everything in their life had been on hold while Kevin was in a coma. Jenny was on stress leave from work and both Mella and Danny had taken several days off school during those days when Jenny wasn't able to get them out of the house in the mornings. All that Kevin could think to say was, "I am going to get better. We'll be fine." Which made him feel better but he thought it probably sounded hollow and unsatisfying to Jenny.

She stayed until the nurse came back in to check on him who then mentioned that he should get some more rest. Kevin looked over at the nurse to signal to her as his eyes were becoming harder to keep open. He could likely go back to sleep again.

Jenny said as she was leaning forward to stand up, "I'll bring the kids and come back to check in after they are out of school."

"Thank you. I hope Mella and Danny aren't too affected when they see me like this." Kevin was already ashamed.

"They came in with me a few times to see you. They'll be much better now you're awake."

Before Jenny walked out Kevin mentioned that he had many emails from the office that he tried scanning through but couldn't focus on them for very long without breaking concentration.

"There are some text messages from Simon saying he needs to see me right away," Kevin added, "but those were from five days ago."

"That's strange, I haven't heard from him and he knew that you were in the hospital without a phone," Jenny explained.

Jenny then told him that everyone in the company knew about the climbing accident by Tuesday morning following the weekend when he arrived in the hospital. When he didn't come in on that Monday after the accident, Simon and Sarah called Jenny before lunch to find out what had happened and then had to put out an email update to inform everyone and keep the morale up.

After Jenny left but before Kevin had drifted off to sleep again, he sent Simon a text to say that he was awake but not moving around yet. Simon texted him back to see if he could meet him at the hospital. Kevin agreed but told him he wouldn't be a very inspiring sight. With two casts and some traction support bracing for his middle back he wasn't mobile other than for his bed folding upwards slightly allowing him to eat.

*****

Simon came into the Hospital to meet with him the next day, late in the afternoon after Kevin finished a few more tests to confirm his brain function was back to normal. Simon gave Kevin an update on what had happened at work while he was in a coma. Hearing what Simon had to say left Kevin on a new level of despair.

Simon stuttered while starting to explain to Kevin the details of how their big new client, GPK

Software, had given them notice they were cancelling
their contract. They had the right to cancel the contract
with shorter notice as they were still in the "trial-phase"
as defined in the agreement. "But then," Simon went
on to say, "we received notice from our next four
biggest clients that they were also terminating their
agreements." At first, he and Sarah didn't understand
what was going on. They soon found out through one
of their close contacts at an older client company who
said all the defecting clients were moving their
contracts to a smaller competitor of theirs. When
Simon told Kevin the name of the other company, it
was one that Kevin was aware of but because they were
so small he never thought of them as a real threat.
Then Simon dropped the bomb that left Kevin as
stunned as he was the first time his face bounced off
the rock during his life-threatening slide.

   After Simon discovered the competing
company's name he checked the website to look at who
their management team was. He saw there were two
new board appointments, "John Williams and (he
hesitated for a moment) Ralph Heinz." Kevin
immediately felt like he was falling again even though
he was safely lying on his bed. Simon then mentioned
that there was also someone new on the management
team. "I think her name is Lauren Williams. Which I
remember because her picture bore a family
resemblance to John who's probably her brother.
Anyway — I hadn't heard of her before but had a
funny feeling I'd seen John's name somewhere and
decided to search my email for it. It turns out he was
cc'd on one of the messages to me and our sales team
because he was part of the executive team at GPK."

   Then Simon divulged the rest of what he knew.

"We think Ralph invested in that little competitor of ours now that he no longer has a stake in Matterhorn. He probably did it with our money too. Then he must have convinced John to move his contract over, probably by giving them an ownership stake for it. The contracts they have taken from us will make them bigger than we will be after all those clients are gone." The news kept getting worse and Kevin was starting to fidget and shift in his bed not able to get comfortable while he listened.

"The revenue from GPK's contract is going to be gone in two weeks, if we can even collect on our final invoices. Then we have three months left of the revenue on the other four contracts. I am sick when I think about what we have to do, Kevin. We are going to have to lay off more than half of our staff," Simon finished. He seemed relieved to share it with Kevin but now looked exhausted.

Kevin couldn't think straight to process everything he was hearing. There was only a single unrelenting thought that kept flashing in his brain like a blinking red light at a four-way stop: pain. The pain was in his body. The pain was in his mind. He had pain for what had already happened and pain from imagining his company starting to unravel.

Turning his head slightly away from Simon to look out the window with his peripheral vision Kevin said, "I need to sleep." Simon sat there for a while before getting up to leave. When he accepted that Kevin wasn't going to respond further he got up and walked towards the door. Simon said something nice but regretful on the way out. Kevin could hear the words but immediately forgot what they were. He didn't want the events to become more real by paying close attention anymore.

Kevin would later think of a short sentence to text to Simon to make sure he knew that he would be coming back. He couldn't think of any details to say regarding a plan or what he thought they should do. Kevin wouldn't admit it, but Simon and Sarah would be on their own at the company for a while to make the best decisions they could. Another two weeks would pass before Kevin recovered enough presence of mind to harness his will power for a purpose.

*****

Almost four weeks after the helicopter ride to the hospital, the imaginary tether of residual pain still kept Kevin confined to his bed most of the time. But at least he was back at home in his own bed, and he was at least able to think and speak with more energy during the day. While his back and leg had not healed enough for him to walk around much other than hobbling to the bathroom or to the kitchen, Kevin started to make more calls and respond to emails.

In his emails, he read that some of the sales team had quit and gone out to work with other companies. One had even gone to work with Ralph at the competing company. That betrayal would never be forgotten. The sales team had said that any prospective client they approached now had heard rumours there was something wrong with their security software. Probably rumours spread by Ralph to help his new investment. The challenge was that all they could do was deny the rumours because there was nothing specific to substantiate them. Unfortunately, because so many clients had left recently and they had already given notice to some of their engineers that they would be laid off, the rumours seemed to be supported by association with Matterhorn Cryptography's decline. The investor that Kevin had brought in to complete the buyout of Ralph's shares was furious. He had heard rumours of what had happened and only received a vague update from Simon who didn't want to say too much because he didn't know the investor well.

They had just received notice over the last day from two more clients saying they were terminating their contracts in three months as well. They still had a small cash reserve in the bank but trying to make decisions on what to do with Matterhorn felt like trying to catch a falling knife. He had asked Simon and Sarah to meet him later on that day at his house to brainstorm what they could do and what decisions they would have to make.

As Simon and Sarah approached the front entrance of the Robertson's house they admired its design. Walking to the house from the turn around at the end of the driveway there was a row of young Japanese maples still growing into the landscape. The ground sloped up towards the front door and a portion of the second storey cantilevered over the front steps with a large grey steel pillar on the opposite side of the walkway holding up the supporting structural beam. The area covered by the second storey provided a sheltered space where guests could look out and admire a view of the city filtered through branches of old growth trees near the front corner of the property. The house looked very new. There was a combination of lightly stained contemporary wood siding and painted smooth exterior walls of some sort of fine-grain stucco. Structural steel members were exposed in different spots around the exterior in a way that tied the segments of the home together with artistic perfection.

Simon pressed the backlit button on the entrance communication panel. They could hear a woman's voice getting louder as it came closer to the other side of the door.

Soon Jenny opened the front door for them to come inside. Jenny led the two of them through the foyer to where Kevin was and they both found comfortable places to sit down in the living room. They hadn't been there before and complimented Jenny on what a great house it was. They were in awe of the architecture and openness around the living room up to the second storey. Even from their seated positions on the couch and chairs in the living room they could see an uninterrupted vista of the entire city. Surrounding the elevated room were floor to ceiling windows with nothing but a thin strip of metal adjoining each pane with the next. The use of light wood continued throughout the interior. The home felt warm and comfortable even though most of the colours on the inside were cool and relaxing.

"Do you want some tea or coffee?" Kevin asked. Both Simon and Sarah declined.

Going straight to the heart of the matter, Sarah started the meeting by saying, "Kevin, you probably don't want to hear this but Simon and I were approached by someone that offered to buy what's left of the company from us. We started exploring valuation with them to determine if their interest was real." Sarah got into the explanation before Simon picked up where she left off to support her.

Simon then added, "the value that we were able to push the buyer to was about 45% of the value for the buyout with Ralph. We are now worried that this is the best we could get. We're struggling to bring on new clients and we could still lose more. The company could shrink to the point where it would take years to sell it and then get out only 20% of what we just put in." Simon was talking quickly by the end and sounded very anxious.

Kevin winced. The last comment about 20% hit him like a kick to the chest but as he leaned backward in response, a shooting pain went through his back from a pinched nerve where his vertebrae were healing. He had already hit his time limit for their problem-solving session.

*****

After all of the unexpected and unmitigated losses Kevin and Jenny had experienced in the last two months, Kevin felt that he was trying very hard to make the best, most rational decisions going forward. He tried to drop the ego he had carried after the buyout and see any personal bias for what it was. The logical thing to do on behalf of the shareholders of the company was always to sell at the best price. That meant selling now before losing even more value. With his vitality only slowly returning he didn't feel he had the strength to land new contracts right away to make up for the ones they'd lost.

Sarah, Simon, and Kevin met one last time to agree to sell Matterhorn Cryptography at the best price they could get. Through the final negotiation with the buyer, the price dropped further to near 30% of the original buyout value. Another client gave notice during negotiation which was a required disclosure as part of their due diligence process. After that, they compromised on any non-financial terms they could to speed the sale along. They had become increasingly nervous and wanted to close it out quickly before anything else went wrong.

Selling Matterhorn was unfortunately the best choice they could have made. Kevin believed he was doing the right thing for the shareholders regardless of what it would mean for him. In the final days leading up to the sale closing, he allowed himself to consider the proceeds he would get from the sale. He didn't have a role to play in the new company because it was going to be swallowed up within a bigger software business and only Sarah was staying with it going forward. The company buying them already had a complete senior management team so Simon and Kevin would be moving on.

Jenny and Kevin had talked the night before the closing about what they would do with their proceeds but all they could agree on was that they would put some money away for the kids' education and hold the rest in savings. They were going to pay down part of the increased mortgage amount but given that Kevin was still not back to full health they thought it was safer to hold cash than to count on getting access to more financing down the road.

Even if they decided to put all of the money against the principal on the mortgage, the lower final sale price didn't provide enough to put a dent in their new larger mortgage payments.

*****

Three months after the cybersecurity company he had founded was sold, Kevin was still looking for a new role he could take on. He was moving around comfortably now although not able to go running and was attending physiotherapy sessions to get his full range of motion back. He was struggling to find a leadership position that would replace the income he had brought home before the accident. All he had picked up so far to keep him busy a couple of days a week were a few limited consulting contracts. In interviews, it was hard for him to wholeheartedly sell himself while knowing he wasn't back to the energy level where he could confidently put out 60-80 hours a week at full speed.

The family finances were being depleted faster than anticipated. Kevin could see where they would start to struggle to make the mortgage payments without cutting down on kids' programs. They had already changed their eating habits with no dinners out at restaurants. The first wake-up call was a few weeks later when they had to choose between being late on the mortgage payment or being late on the car payment.

In the evening after dinner one night when the kids finished eating and left the kitchen Jenny couldn't hold in the stress any longer.

"If we use up our savings to make our car and mortgage payments and we still don't make enough income to cover it all then we will lose everything." Jenny's voice was raised but not quite to a shouting volume.

"I am working on getting a better job, Jenny. Do you think I wanted to go through any of the things that happened?" Kevin became defensive.

"We can't keep hoping every month. In three more months, our savings will be gone and then what?" Jenny's momentum was building as she unleashed her thoughts. "I don't want to get stuck and be forced to move but have nowhere to go. I won't let the kids go through that."

"Ok, I don't want that either but I am sure we will be fine." Kevin was trying to stay in the debate but wasn't saying anything concrete.

"How?" Jenny kept pushing.

"What's going to change?" She asked again.

"Do we have to sell the house?" Jenny started each question before Kevin could even think of a response.

"What else can we even do?" When she said it aloud, it was the first time Kevin had ever let the idea of selling the house enter his mind.

Kevin had bought and sold a handful of houses. In the past he'd found when buying or selling a home that had been lived in by other people, once the money was received after the sale, he was ready to move on and forget about the house. This home was different. He and Jenny had put hundreds of hours into the design and materials selection process not to mention the time and battle initially involved in getting the building lot. The approvals from the city were also a test of patience and resilience. When Jenny first talked about building the home, she described getting settled in it as the last time they were ever going to move. Kevin thought that with the juggling he had to do for the financing, coupled with selling the rental property which he had owned since before he and Jenny were married, he should be the one who felt more attachment to their home. Then he started to see that for Jenny it was a place for the family. Everything about it was designed with all four of them in mind. It even had an extra bedroom neatly in line with the other two kids' rooms, waiting for another baby to come along.

All of that time spent planning and dreaming about how their lives would unfold had left out the expectation that life can be surprising in unimaginable ways.

"I don't know Jenny. I hate the idea of selling this house." Kevin was avoiding the necessary answer. At the same time he started to visualize what moving to some other place would be like, knowing it could never match this home they had built together.

Kevin was no longer making eye contact with her and had withdrawn from the conversation. He was still stuck in the past. He knew she couldn't, wouldn't, let the kids suffer. It wasn't even a possibility for her that the kids wouldn't have a home with a back yard and their friends nearby.

"There is no stability or predictability in our lives. We have to make sure our two kids are safe Kevin," Jenny said to him.

Kevin thought she was speaking specifically about the two they had to the exclusion of the idea that they could have another. He wondered why she had never brought up the topic of having another baby. He didn't need to talk about it anyway because it was too painful to consider given what they had just gone through. Since the accident, every time he got close to her it was just a reminder of their whole world shattering. He thought they she had gone from wondering if he was going to recover from the coma to wondering if they would be able to cover the monthly payments on their family home.

Kevin then felt like he was in two pits at the same time. A money pit and a marriage pit. He didn't know how he was going to get out of either of them but he needed to figure out how to stop digging.

Chapter 4
The Family Home

The day the real estate agent pounded the upright post of the 'for sale' sign into the corner of the lot between the shrubs, Kevin knew selling the house was a fait accompli.

"This is all screwed up," Kevin said under his breath looking out at the front yard with the sign standing there staring back at him. It was like an advertisement to all of his neighbours and anyone who drove by that he had failed. He hadn't been able to look after his family. He hadn't been able to provide as a husband. Now, what could he do? He stood there looking out the main window in the living room.

A financial loss was always talked about as something that happened in an instant. Like how a judgement is delivered for a lawsuit. There is hope until there isn't and then the receipt of the decision provides for an instantaneous result. Seeing the family income deteriorate and then finally being forced to sell the home was painstakingly slow torture. Even selling the home wouldn't be quick. Getting a home like theirs ready to go on the market was no small task and the process of waiting for a real offer to come in could take months. They had already started looking for a place to rent to get a sense of what was available. It was

going to be tough to find something near the kids'
school that would have enough room for them all.

Homes were renting quickly so they couldn't
commit to a place until their home was contracted to
be sold with an unconditional offer. Then they would
have to scramble to get the next suitable place that
came available.

"Moving out of this place was never supposed
to happen," Kevin thought to himself. "The last time I
had to sell the family home was to move in here. When
we completed construction, I told myself that would be
the last time we would ever have to move our stuff
with a truck."

*****

When the home sold it turned out the bank's
appraiser had been unusually aggressive on the value
for the home. The mortgage worked out to just over
91% of the proceeds they got from the sale (after the
costs of selling it). They decided to sell because if they
defaulted on the mortgage and the bank started a
foreclosure process they would likely get nothing.
Somehow court-ordered sales never seem to fetch
prices much higher than the debt owed (if that) after all
the legal costs involved.

With what was left from the sale and their
family income being lower than it was before, they
wouldn't be able to buy again for some time and
certainly not in the neighbourhood where they had
built their dream home.

The good news, if it could be called that, was
that they did find a home near the kids' school that was
big enough. It had recently been sold through
foreclosure and was picked up by a younger couple,

Frank and Louise Wild, who had decided to become real estate investors. They had done a little cosmetic clean up on it but not a lot. Their 'for rent' ad had been up for only a day when Jenny spotted it. Jenny rushed over and was able to get a deposit in on the rental home the day before their sale went unconditional. Jenny was silently relieved that they now had a place to live in they could afford. It accommodated their kids and that was enough.

One point of silent contention about the house was that it only had three bedrooms. It had a den too but it was shy of being adaptable for a fourth bedroom. The den could work for the odd guest to stay on a small fold out mattress but it couldn't work as a third child's bedroom. It was really more of an alcove off the dining room than an actual room with a door. When Jenny said the house would work for them, she and Kevin both looked at the summary on the rental listing and thought the same thing about the size of their family without saying it. Jenny was anxious to lock down a place for their current family needs and they hadn't seen many options come available.

The rental house was average in almost every way other than its location. The street was part of a great neighbourhood. After they moved in Kevin noticed all sorts of strange things the prior occupant had done to the home. The basement was largely unfinished and given it was a rental there was nothing much that they could do with it other than store all of their extra stuff there. Things they found in the house caused them to wonder if the people who had been living there during the foreclosure had succumbed to the stress of losing their home. It seemed as though they developed an obsession with hanging things. There were nails and nail holes everywhere. There were unused doors in the basement that someone had painted names on —presumably the individual family members' first names. There were dozens of different colours of paint and some rooms in the house looked like they had been painted several times where paint drips or overlap showed layers of different colours. In many places, the trim hadn't ever been painted at all and was still bare unfinished wood.

There was a very strange addition to the attic of the home that created the third bedroom. The addition was lopsided and the room didn't have a full height ceiling. Kevin would have to duck every time he went through into that room. When moving furniture into the house he kept smacking his forehead against the door jam. After the third time hitting his head on the frame, Kevin swore loudly and kicked the bottom of the door, creating a crack from the bottom hinge out to the middle of the door panel. Thankfully Danny wanted to take that room, at his age he was still short enough for the height of the door frame and the ceiling not to bother him.

This was a strange house with a mediocre interior and lots of deferred maintenance. It would take some time getting used to, and even after the first month there, it felt like visiting their grandparents when pulling into the driveway. Between its vintage and the unsettling memories the house was connected to, it just didn't feel like coming home.

*****

After they had been there for several weeks the new reality of their lives had started to sink in and Kevin realized a coldness was growing between him and Jenny. The kids didn't seem to mind the house, apparently, they didn't feel the loss like Jenny and Kevin did. The kids did make the odd comment about missing their old bedroom, missing the hot tub, or missing the bigger yard. Even though normally people would call their prior home their "old house", because of the style of the home they had just moved out of and the condition of where they were now living, the kids got into calling the rental home the "old home" and the other one the "new house." Whenever they would refer to something they missed about it they would always start with, "remember at our new house, how we had…"

Early one evening when Kevin would normally be still at work at Matterhorn, he and Jennifer were in the kitchen attending to dinner preparations. Kevin's schedule was more sporadic now so he found himself at home more often.

"Can you watch the kids when they get home from school tomorrow?" Jenny briskly asked Kevin, in a tone that almost dared him not to say yes.

"Ah, sure. No problem." Kevin said.

"I have to go out after work and get a couple of things," Jenny said ambiguously but firmly, not inviting further discussion.

"Okay yeah, of course." Kevin felt like she was stressed about something but he couldn't exactly pin down what it could be or if it was his fault. It seemed like she was carrying resentment or some aggravation she didn't want to share.

Each of them were then back in their own heads again. Carrying on with the meal prep without speaking.

Kevin thought about the experience of transitioning into this old house. In the end, the final steps of selling their dream home and moving into the rental had all been a blur. Like operating on autopilot, both Jenny and Kevin checked off all the items on their to-do lists and then one day woke up in a familiar bed but in an unfamiliar room. The house smelled like moth balls in all the closets with a dry dusty wood tinge that occasionally wafted through the air. Once they got everything into the rental home, the friction between the two of them was beginning to build around every normal daily interaction. However, neither of them could articulate the fundamental issue. When they looked at each other now, did they see someone different? Did they see each other as the person they had married or was it someone new staring back?

Living in a rented home was not something that Kevin had experienced since the end of the year after finishing his university degree. He had been keen to get into the real estate market and started with the purchase of a little townhouse, but instead of moving into it, he rented it out. Beginning with that one he spring-boarded into buying a home he could move into. Later, after meeting Jenny and getting engaged, they would rent out that second house and sell the townhouse to ultimately buy the home where they started a family. They lived in the family home until deciding to build their dream home when Kevin's business became a success story. Looking back, he had managed his own rental properties longer than he had lived in a rental home himself.

It was shocking to see how much the price of rent had gone up over the years. Since they had moved into the home they built, Kevin hadn't been following the rental market closely. He didn't have time to watch anything other than his growing software company in those years. Not only had rent gone up but it seemed like the quality of homes available for rent had gone down. Kevin wondered if perhaps all of the other homes that had previously been rentals had appreciated in value enough for the landlords to sell them to homeowners and put their investment into something else. That would leave only older, more poorly maintained homes that were sold cheaply enough that investors felt it was worthwhile to bring them back into the rental market. The numbers seemed to be harder to make work as far as investing in rental property was concerned even with the rental rates going up.

What Kevin soon came to realize was how frustrating it was being a tenant in a home he had no control of. He couldn't decide to renovate or make changes even for something as simple as painting the kids' bedrooms. Those things were someone else's decision. And even if he wanted to, it didn't make sense for him to spend even $100 improving the home on the inside or on the landscaping, because every dollar he spent beyond his monthly rent was a complete waste of money. He would see nothing for it. Having been a homeowner so long he already had the habit of maintaining the yard, so he mowed the lawn and did some yard work which the Wilds appreciated. The thing was, he didn't feel the need to mow it as often as he would if it were his own home. It was a strange mindset for him to have after questioning why his own tenants in the past would never really take care of his rental properties the way he thought they should. He was somewhere between apathy and downright spite for the fact that he was living in someone else's property.

Kevin had never really been that interested in real estate other than what he needed to know for the two rental properties he had over the years. Since being forced to move out of their dream home and into this rental, he had started to pay a lot closer attention to any news about real estate or mortgages. He received a crash course in what he could do, or in his current situation what he couldn't do, when it came time to get a new mortgage approved. He started watching news relating to the city's housing market and the appreciation in the value of homes in his neighbourhood. There was lots of media coverage and ongoing talk about how difficult it was becoming for people to buy a home. Home prices kept going up and mortgage rules seemed to change regularly in ways that made it harder for people to qualify for a loan. People who were already in a home seemed to be fine but anyone who didn't already own was struggling to get into the market.

He felt like he had the chops to understand real estate after building a cybersecurity software company but some aspects were either conflicting or based on inaccessible credit data. Some of the banks' policies felt like a concealed black box used to protect their reputation or retain negotiating leverage. They always preferred to make it the client's fault that they didn't fit a lending policy following a change rather than try to come up with new credit products in whatever form was feasible for as many people as possible.

"After all of the turmoil that has happened to my family," Kevin was thinking to himself, "if I could figure out a way to get us back in control of the roof over our heads, maybe it will help me regain more than just the lost wealth." Kevin had started to lose confidence in himself but didn't think Jenny saw it. He couldn't tell though if it was affecting his interaction with her. Every day now brought similar thoughts. "How to get back what was lost? What was it going to take to find their spark again? How could they buy a home again?"

*****

Every day brought more of the same. It was a repetitive mindset that wouldn't relent.

"If I can only get us back to what we had a year ago." Kevin kept revisiting it in his mind. "I have to figure out a way to rewind the clock to before the shotgun clause was used against me."

Kevin often thought of strategies or ideas on how to build a new company. However, those seemed further out of his reach. The more pressing need was to increase the family's equity stake to get back into homeownership again. Sitting at his desk in the basement while taking a break from the last consulting project, he looked down to see his phone start sliding across the desk. It's ringer was off but the smooth cover and the vibrations from silent mode made it hover on the desk like an air hockey puck. It was mid-afternoon and the call was coming from Jenny. It was too early for her to have picked up Mella and Danny from school already. Kevin picked up the phone to answer the call.

"Hi, ...she said what?!" Kevin was shocked. He had barely said hello before Jenny started a rant about why she was called into Mella's school.

Mella had become much more resistant than usual in the mornings when it was time to get in the car to go to school. Jenny and Kevin had both noticed her becoming adversarial when trying to get her out the door in the morning. The more they concentrated on getting out in time for the school bell, the more resistant she would become. It was much more than the normal dislike for school all kids seem to share. She would plant her feet against the sides of the door if they tried to carry her out. If that didn't work she would grab the doorframe with her fingertips on the way by or even start pounding on Kevin's back if he was carrying her out. Any pressure to get out the door quickly just made it worse. Twice in the last two weeks, she had broken down into tears the moment she got into the car after school. She was in grade five now. Her birthday fell early in the year which meant she was one of the older kids in her grade but still had a childish look of innocence. That being so, no one at her school, whether it be teachers or other kids, would ever look at her as an innocent little 11-year-old girl after what she had just done.

"That is insane," Kevin stammered, still reeling from Jenny's summary of events.

As it turned out, Mella had been ignoring her teacher's instructions and doing so in a vocal way that was disturbing kids who sat near her in class. After multiple frustrating experiences, Mr. Davis, her teacher, had tried to create some discipline by asking for help from the principal, Ms. Stewart. A few days earlier, the principal had pulled Mella out of class and taken her down to the administrative offices to sit alone for a while. Today, however, when it happened again and the teacher called the office with the phone in the classroom to ask for the principal, Mella overheard him. As Ms. Stewart walked into the classroom, Mella said in a defiant and perfectly articulated way while looking straight at the principal, "Oh, did you come to give Mr. Davis a blow job?"

Jenny then went on to describe the experience of meeting with the principal to hear all of this. Jenny was a protective mother, and Kevin could hear from her voice that she didn't take any shit from the other woman. Even if Jenny felt embarrassed as a parent, she didn't let it show. She used the position that the school was ignoring the best practices that both the education assistant and behavioural consultant working with Mella had advised them of.

Kevin, on the other hand, knew he would be embarrassed going into the school after that. He was thinking that all of the teachers would know about this within a day. From that day on they wouldn't be able to help themselves; they would judge him and Jenny as parents.

Jenny finished her retelling of events with a little dig.

"I was looking at Ms. Stewart while she was describing Mella's outburst," she said. "Ms. Stewart's body language made me think she didn't find Mr. Davis unattractive. Just that in her words, what Mella said was 'disgustingly inappropriate.' It wouldn't surprise me if Mella heard Mr. Davis flirting with Ms. Stewart at some point and assumed it meant they had already gotten together. Who knows what these teachers do after the school bell rings."

Jenny was visibly furious with the entire episode. Angry at Mella, angry at the school teachers, and angry that she was once again dealing with more chaos.

*****

In the aftermath of what they would call the "naughtiness" incident, a double entendre for Mella's outburst and what they suspected Mella's teacher and the school principal were up to after school hours, Kevin started to associate some of the kids' new behaviour with the turmoil of moving. There had been strain on the family during everything they had experienced. That association didn't alleviate his circular thoughts from continually reminding him of the need for stability at home.

What could they do about their home and getting back into ownership even though their income didn't qualify them for a regular mortgage? They had enough income to make their monthly rent payments but still didn't have a downpayment. Jenny decided to go from working 3/4 time which had allowed her to be around for the kids more, up to full-time hours. She'd be working with the team that was reviewing the hospital's plan to build new surgical suites, and would even be taking some overtime hours. She said she couldn't leave their income up to chance. Kevin's hopes of building a new business and re-establishing a greater level of income again were fleeting. She was going to have to see it to believe in it. There was no way she was going to let the unpredictable nature of Kevin's work take away from her being able to sleep at night by knowing they had food and rent covered.

As more time went by they got to know Frank and Louise, the couple who owned the home they were renting. Jenny learned they were trying to start a family and if they did, would want to move into that rental home themselves. The home they were living in at the moment was quite small and didn't have enough room for a growing family. Their goal, which was not dissimilar to Kevin's original approach, was to rent out their bigger home and live in the smaller one until the family needed more space. Frank and Louise Wild bought the house for the same reason that Jenny spotted it as an option for their family: it was in a great neighbourhood and close to the kids' school.

Now the problem of needing to buy a home again was heating back up. It would immediately hit a roaring boil and need to be moved to the front burner if Louise got pregnant. The momentary financial stability that Kevin and Jenny felt when they moved into the rental house was now overshadowed by a pending threat based on when their landlords found out they would be expecting.

What if he could find a real estate owner who eventually wanted to sell their rental property but didn't have an exact date they needed to sell it? What if he agreed to take care of all of the maintenance, which he would prefer to do anyway since landlords never really looked after their rental properties — funny how that worked. Neither the landlords nor the tenants had an incentive to keep the properties in great shape because it would cost both parties more. Kevin decided he would keep thinking about it and try to figure something out.

*****

After finishing a consulting mandate at a client's office in the early afternoon one day, Kevin was walking around with a bounce in his step and a relaxed grin on his face, and he decided to buy Jenny some flowers along with her favourite chocolates. It was a clear sunny day and he felt that it would be good to show her some appreciation for all her hard work and enduring the new "normal" they'd become accustomed to. He arrived home before she did. Hoping to surprise her he sent her a text saying he would pick up the kids from the after-school program so that she would expect him to be out. He stayed at home to wait for her, planning to go for the kids near the end of the pick-up window.

Jenny got home and walked over to the counter where the flowers were sitting in a vase. As she was picking up the package of chocolate, Kevin walked up behind her and leaned down to kiss her neck. Without thinking she shrugged down her shoulder and moved away from him as a defensive reflex, startled by his presence. Thinking he had just surprised her and that she simply wasn't expecting him home, Kevin stretched his arms out to embrace her. Jenny pushed back with what looked like reluctance to Kevin.

"What's up Jenny?" Kevin said, thinking that it sounded more confrontational than he intended. "I had a good day, finished the latest project and wanted to bring home some of your favourite flowers — white lilies."

"It's been a long day. A lot is going on at work," Jenny responded, not giving up any ground.

"This isn't the first time that you seemed like you didn't want to have anything to do with me." Kevin let out some of his frustration. All he could focus on was that she'd been overly dismissive lately.

"What do you want from me?" she said submissively, which he thought meant that she didn't care about what the outcome of the conversation was.

"I don't know Jenny, it just seems like we aren't even connected anymore. We live together, and we cooperate looking after the kids, but that's about it," Kevin said and waited for a response.

Jenny didn't say anything back right away. At first, Kevin thought it may have been the first time she had considered that description of their relationship but he was so worked up at that point he couldn't stop himself.

"Do you even want to be with me anymore, to be married anymore?" Kevin let it out.

It was the thing he had wondered in a moment of weakness but wanted to force the issue to find some relief from the question that had been bouncing around in his head.

Jenny looked stunned to hear him say something like that after everything they'd been through. She didn't say anything back. She had a stoic look on her face, her lips clenched together and her eyebrows straight and unwavering. She alternated between looking down at the floor and looking out the window past Kevin's shoulder.

"I don't know what to say to you," she said, turning to look at his face for a split second, and then walked out of the room. Before her back was to him Kevin could see the muscles in her jaw were clenched and her mouth was set firmly in a line. Her eyebrows were tense and drawn down.

Watching her back as she left the room, waiting for her to say something, Kevin felt even worse for trying to voice his worries for what was happening to them.

Without hearing any definitive answer from her he felt even less certainty that everything was going to work out between the two of them. Given that she didn't deny his question, it was even harder now for him to ignore his fear that he was losing her.

He left to get the kids, and was fidgeting with his keys while driving, stirred up but still resolved to do whatever he could to make up for losing their home. He had no clarity on what was going to happen with their relationship but with his teeth locked together tightly, he kept his mind concentrated on seeing it through.

*****

Kevin sat at his desk thinking after the kids had gone to sleep. What other ideas had he not considered to solve their homeownership problem? Living in a rented home had made him very much aware of the problems facing renters: being unable to make high-quality repairs or even cosmetic changes, the risk that they would have to move if the landlord had other plans for the home, the inability to save a down payment while making high monthly rent payments, and the frustration of seeing homeownership slip further out of reach every month as home prices increased faster than he could save.

He tried to think of some benefits of renting that he could perhaps turn to his advantage, and found himself thinking about his days as a landlord. There were challenges to that role, too. Being a landlord required a sizeable and long-term investment of capital. There were maintenance costs, there was tenant turnover and the difficulty finding reliable tenants, and the risk of losing income if the unit was empty for a month or two or three. There was also the wear and tear on properties over time as tenants never really took care of the place, and sometimes outright damage from careless or vindictive tenants.

Kevin had been lucky with one of his previous properties, and had a reliable, long-term tenant who took reasonably good care of the place. That had made being a landlord a little easier, and gave him some peace of mind.

Then he thought, what if we sign a long-term rental agreement? Then we could stay in the home for five to seven years. And if we still couldn't get a mortgage to buy it then, have an agreement with the landlord where we got a share of its increased value over the time we lived there? We would have to live in the home up to when it was sold, of course, like we would have if we owned it. Then we could use our share plus our savings to go and buy a new home like a condo when the kids are ready to go off to college.

Thinking further, he then realized the landlord had no motivation to share any of the increase in the value. What would the owner get out of the long-term lease that would be worth trading a share for?

Stuck on that question and not able to come up with an answer, he wrote a few lines in his black moleskin notebook. It was where he liked to record his important thoughts. As he stood up, ready to go to bed, an idea came to mind.

What if he set up the contract so that he was legally responsible for all of the repairs to the home, all of the maintenance and the insurance deductible for any claim? What if the multi-year agreement that gave him and Jenny the security of knowing they would have the home for a long time and wouldn't be kicked out on short notice, also gave the landlord something?

Kevin was remembering back to when he had his rental property and how much time he spent looking after the home. He had even tried hiring a property manager once and then realized how much it cost to have a middle-man contracting out all the maintenance. Especially when the middle-man had to hire separate trades people for every repair regardless of how big or small it was.

As a long-term tenant, if he did everything himself, or in the worst-case scenario asked a friend or two to help if something big came up, it would cost him very little to maintain the home. Although, it would save the landlord hundreds of dollars a month and potentially thousands of dollars a year. Then, with a long-term rental agreement, no property manager would be needed because there would never be a vacancy and the landlord wouldn't have to worry about re-renting the property. Effectively, Kevin would be treating the home like any homeowner would, and why not? If he had a share of the increase in value he would make sure it was looked after to help the value improve as much as possible.

If the tenant had a share in the value of the home, then the tenant's goals and the landlord's goals would be aligned. As the tenant's share of the value grew then the tenant would have something to lose which would mean a greater pride in the condition of the home.

It seemed like it was close to making sense but still not quite compelling. After writing down a few more ideas he was tired enough to fall asleep, and dropped it for the night.

*****

Two days later Kevin got the first good news he could remember in what seemed like forever. One of the recent consulting clients he had worked with had a senior executive position open up and they had asked him to come in to discuss their plans. He assumed they had meant to have him fill in the gaps until they found someone new but instead offered him the position. It felt great to be recognized as a candidate to help lead the company. It wasn't the CEO role so he was comfortable he could handle it but it still wasn't near the level of income that he had before. He wasn't sure if he was ready to run the gauntlet yet and take on the top spot as chief executive. He felt he may still have a blind spot after what had happened. He was still unsettled by the clients of his company leaving to go to the competing company Ralph owned.

It was great news for the family though. It would provide a consistent income to make it easier to budget and plan around. Jenny had to feel better about that, at least he thought she would.

Getting home that night Kevin walked in the door standing straight up with his head held high and a relaxed expression on his face. It would be a few weeks before the new role would be confirmed. When it did he wanted to get back to the bank to find out what amount of mortgage his new income would qualify them for. Then once his new employment agreement was signed they could get back to saving up a downpayment. He kept thinking about the idea of sharing part of the value of the rental home to help them shorten the amount of time it would take to build-up their downpayment. He was in an optimistic mood and believed that in another five years his income would improve further and he could buy a house again if they could save up enough for the purchase.

He decided to explain to Jenny his new idea of sharing the increase in value of a home. The first time he tried to describe it to her she wasn't sure about it. She couldn't see Frank and Louise, the couple they were currently renting their home from, agreeing to it given they wanted eventually move in themselves. Jenny was reluctant to get excited about it. His new job wasn't confirmed, she didn't want to move again, and she didn't have the experience renting properties that he did. She just couldn't get her head around how it would work from the landlord's point of view. Kevin realized something was missing and didn't try to convince Jenny

of anything yet. He was just happy to have something
to talk about that could be positive for them. Jenny
preferred to not put hope in things if they didn't seem
likely to happen. She had to look out for the kids. Only
things that were real today were worth believing in.

*****

      That night while lying in bed, all Kevin could
think about was how much he was still attracted to
Jenny. He adored her curves and loved looking into her
eyes, only he noticed she wouldn't make eye contact
with him nearly as often recently. For a moment he
suspended disbelief in the idea that their relationship
was struggling and put his hand on her shoulder. He
wanted to see if she was still awake. He couldn't see if
her eyes were closed as she was lying on her side facing
away from him.

      After rubbing the back of her shoulder with his
thumb, she moved her arm back and rested her hand
on the side of his leg just above the knee, like she used
to do to remind him when they were trying to get
pregnant at that right time of the month. Kevin
thought that was a good sign so he moved his hand
down over her arm to lightly rub her nipple. In a few
moments it had perked up and she started to fidget
with her legs. Jenny quickly turned to kiss him and
started to push his shorts down.

      Kevin was surprised by how fast she had
responded. His astonishment wasn't going to slow him
down though, and he certainly didn't need more
enticement to be fully and completely ready to respond.
Jenny started to slide her waistband down and Kevin
helped her to kick off her pyjamas all the while still
kissing each other. It had been long enough since they

had been intimate so some of the sensations felt new again.

Without taking her shirt off she tugged on the side of his ribs to move him over on top of her. Pressing her cheek into his, she reached down to help to get him started. Her body was heating up and she flung the blankets down Kevin's back. For a brief period while they were lost in the moment, it felt to him like they were back on their wedding night. All the recent strife was gone. The image of her coming over to him with her wedding dress still on blinked into his mind. His eyes were closed and their bodies were as close now as they'd ever been. That image lasted only a little while.

They were both speechless, their chests heaving with every rapidly taken breath. Jenny reached forwards to grab the side of his legs just below the hips, pulling him in, willing him to go faster. Kevin was uncontrollably enjoying it, thrilled with how she had come on once they'd started. Kevin tried shifting a few different times in an attempt to prolong the intensity but he had hit his threshold and could no longer hold back. Jenny hugged him around his ribs and held him tight before they both relaxed.

"That was great. You were great," Kevin said quietly. Jenny made a move like she was finished too, although Kevin was certain she hadn't. He wasn't sure that she even tried fully, almost like she was looking for it to be over quicker by pushing Kevin to climax as fast as possible.

After they had got their clothes back on and gotten settled in bed again, Jenny seemed to nod off right away. Kevin's heart was still beating too fast for him to fall asleep so he got comfortable lying on his side with his eyes closed. As he started to calm down a fleeting thought entered his mind that Jenny was proving to him they were still married. Her fast response was her way of showing him that he had wrongly questioned if she still wanted to be with him. He had hoped she would make love to him because she wanted to and not because she felt obligated. It was the first time they had made love that turned out to be just sex.

Kevin knew then he'd made up none of the lost ground.

It was going to take more. At that moment he couldn't have understood what lay ahead. It wouldn't be a simple exercise, a five step process, or follow a clearly defined path.

Not knowing what else he could do he started to wonder if it would take far more than he was willing to admit to overcome the pain they'd experienced. Kevin tried to imagine something more significant he could do as he was drawn into the darkness of slumber.

Chapter 5
SOMETHING NEW

It was all over the news in the morning...

Sometime after midnight two nurses were standing outside the hospital elevator waiting for the doors to open while talking about a patient they were dealing with. The doors opened and they walked inside to head down to the main level. As the elevator started its descent, they heard a deep rumble throughout the building, then the power blinked off and the main lights in the elevator cab went dark. The automatic brakes locked and the elevator stopped immediately but no backup lighting came on and they didn't hear an alarm sound. They were in total darkness.

Five minutes before the nurses entered the elevator the night maintenance crew was working away on their normal rotation. Harold (who everyone called Harry) was cleaning and inspecting the tank room where the supply of medical gas tanks and equipment for the research facility was stored at the hospital. As he was turning to leave the hard edge on his equipment cart hit the side of a valve on one of the tanks and cracked it. It happened to be an acetylene gas tank that had been misplaced within the rack for the oxygen tanks. This particular tank was also due to be recycled and had a faulty valve but presently it was full. After

Harry's cart knocked into it there was a moment where it teetered back and forth threatening to fall. When Harry pulled the equipment cart back, he caught the restraint strap holding the tanks in and pulled it loose. The tank with the damaged valve fell, breaking the valve clean off, and it sparked against the concrete floor igniting the acetylene and causing it to explode. The explosion of the smaller tank caused a chain reaction with the rest of the tanks lined up where it had fallen. The cascading explosions spread and ignited other chemicals stored in the same room. Some of the chemicals spread the fire that was fed by all of the oxygen tanks which were compromised in the explosion.

Harry was first thrown back against the cinder block wall by the concussive blast knocking him out cold. His life was extinguished before he would ever regain consciousness, as the intensity of the chemical fire consumed him.

With the outdated design of the building, the explosion and heat from the fire destroyed a main power supply conduit that ran from the backup power system as well as the connection lines for that wing of the hospital's fire alarm monitoring system. Everyone on shift that night reacted after experiencing the rumble in the building simultaneously with the lights going out. All health and safety systems are required to be connected to backup power but somehow the explosion disconnected part of the monitoring system for that wing. The fire department got an automatic notification but couldn't figure out what was happening because the sensors got cut off in the explosion. Staff were immediately on with the fire department while the nearest night time crew at the station scrambled to get into the truck and get over to the hospital.

The fire created enough smoke to make half a floor uninhabitable along with all the rooms stacked up on that end of the building. The seasonally warm weather made most hospital inhabitants keep their windows open. As the smoke rose up along the outside wall it curled in through the openings and blackened the white ceiling squares.

The two nurses caught in the elevator were stuck there until the fire rescue team was able to get in and pry open the doors to evacuate them. Luckily they were not hurt and none of the patients in any of the rooms had been hurt other than some minor smoke inhalation. There was a flurry of activity to move the patients around within the hospital to other rooms unaffected by the fire once the fire chief had confirmed the threat of it spreading was eliminated. Luckily the tank storage room also had an exterior door that was used by the fire crew to suppress the source of the flames quickly upon their arrival. Their water hoses had little effect to start with so they quickly switched to chemical suppressants. The small room off the end of the hospital was completely enclosed in thick white foam like a blizzard had blown a snow drift up on that corner of the building.

Watching the news coverage Kevin heard a reporter say, "We don't know when they will get the main power supply reconnected back on to all wings of the hospital and the emergency response group from the fire department is not commenting on how many people may be seriously injured or worse right now. As you can see behind where I am standing there is still black smoke rising from the storage room where the fire started although the flames have been brought under control…" Kevin saw Jenny walk across the corner of the TV slightly out of focus in the news coverage on her way to enter the building with someone wearing an emergency response jacket. He shut off the TV. He would get the details from Jenny when he spoke with her next. He just had no idea when that would be.

*****

Jenny had immediately received messages from the night shift administrative staff at the hospital so she left home to go to the hospital after the emergency response teams had arrived. She got there early while the fire crews were finishing their inspections and documenting what they needed for their reports. The camera crews for the local media correspondents had arrived just after her. When she knew everything was under control, she sent a message to Kevin to let him know the place was in a state of anarchy that she'd never seen before, but the patients were now safe.

"We are getting everyone moved around but there is way too much to do. I doubt I will make it home before 10 pm tonight." Jenny messaged Kevin just after 6 am.

"OK. Good luck today. Do you want me to bring you lunch?" Kevin responded back.

"No need. We are going to have food brought in for everyone here so…" She had sent the message without finishing it and the display on the phone showed that she was still typing. Kevin waited a few minutes but nothing further came back.

Jenny must have been distracted and didn't get back to finish the text until later that evening while eating dinner at her desk before returning to work. Everyone at the hospital was frantically working to figure out how to fit all of the patients into rooms untouched by smoke. They started immediately moving all equipment out of the areas that would need to be cleaned up and restored. It would be an outright sprint to get the hospital fully functioning as soon as possible once the investigation into the event surrounding the explosion was completed.

Over the following days Kevin could see that Jenny was as exhausted as he had been from the shotgun clause experience. The lost use of space at the hospital, the repair to the safety systems, and restoration of the smoke damage created havoc for Jenny's schedule. Her days had already been busy with her additional workload which would now be more hectic as the hospital's fundraising campaign kicked into high gear, along with the planning phase for the new state-of-the-art surgical suites. Jenny's team was deeply involved in budgeting and procurement for the new equipment and staffing that would be required, and she was working lots of overtime. Her team was directly responsible for all of those aspects of the hospital's operation. It was a huge project that took a lot of her energy.

Kevin offered to help in any way he could but his assistance amounted to looking after the kids more while Jenny was away from the family dealing with the project. When Jenny was preoccupied with work, Kevin decided he would keep working to resolve their housing issue.

Whatever solution would put a roof over their heads long term, he needed to find it soon. Kevin received final confirmation for his new full-time role and signed the agreement. It would be more money on average than his consulting mandates had brought in and it was consistent, which was even more important for the family.

When he went to meet with the bank, however, he was disappointed again. He found out it was still too early for him to use his new income. The expense-reduced self-employment income he had been earning most recently was all that showed up on his tax return and it wasn't enough for the bank.

Sitting back in his basement office, he rehashed the idea of a multi-year home rental agreement. Using his experience from building the software company, Kevin started forecasting how much the landlord would make with his value sharing idea. He entered details for the property management and all home maintenance and the benefit of eliminating vacancy expenses. He then looked at how much equity he would accumulate with different amounts of shared growth in the value of the home as well as the principal repayment of the mortgage.

There still seemed to be something missing. He wouldn't build up equity in the home fast enough to get to the point where he would be able buy the home. "What if I save a little more each month towards the equity — effectively paying the landlord each month for a small amount of the equity already in the property?" Kevin thought.

Something amazing jumped out of the page at him. All of sudden by adding in $150 to $375 per month to the equity build-up, his equity in the property would grow fast enough to allow him to buy the home in as little as three years and build more than enough equity for the purchase within five to seven years, with a greater variety of mortgage alternatives.

The kicker was that now when he looked at the cash flow for the landlord, the whole idea made sense.

He remembered the rental properties he had and thought he would love to be a landlord for tenants using his new multi-year shared value agreement.

"Maybe I will explore acquiring another rental property in the future again? Well, first things first," Kevin thought to himself.

Reviewing his forecast, there was great positive cash flow every month and from the property landlord's point of view it was a very easy investment to manage. With the tenant motivated to look after the maintenance of the home in exchange for a share of the value, it greatly reduces the management expense and reduces the time required for looking after the rental property. If he set up an automatic electronic payment every month then it would become a very easy investment for a real estate investor to look after.

Kevin summarized the benefits for both parties by sharing growth in the equity value of the home. The tenant received a share of the home appreciation, a share of the mortgage pay-down, and the accumulation of equity from a simple savings plan connected to the very home they lived in. The landlord benefited from having an alignment of interests with the tenant because the tenant took care of maintaining the home like it was their own, the tenant paid the monthly savings amount to the landlord as a reimbursement for a small part of the equity the landlord had to put up to buy the home in the first place, and because the tenant signed a long-term rental agreement the landlord no longer needed a property manager and wouldn't have vacancy issues or the marketing cost of re-renting the property.

"This opportunity should be easy to get people excited about. Great return on investment. Complete legal control of the property. No management headaches." Kevin thought. And from what he remembered from his own experience, the landlord would still enjoy helpful tax write-offs.

"What would be the right percentage share of appreciation that would make sense to the landlord?" Kevin said it aloud while leaning back in his chair with his finger and thumb held up to his closed lips, deeply concentrating.

If he were willing to do everything to maintain the property, eliminate the need for any property management, eliminate vacancy expenses and lost revenue, and provide the equity contribution each month, how much could the landlord share before it was no longer worth it for them?

Being comfortable with coding, he decided to build a simple algorithm. He thought that it could be turned into a formalized software program to make the calculations automatically if other people wanted to use it too.

Running the algorithm with different assumptions Kevin found the investor could give up a 34% share of the growth in value in some circumstances and still be better off than if they had shared-nothing, foregone the additional cash flow, and covered all of the traditional maintenance and management costs themselves.

From Kevin's point of view, if he got at least 20% of the growth in equity as a tenant, then as the property value went up and the mortgage balance was paid down, he would get closer and closer to a conventional down payment. This worked even if the home's market value went up significantly. He would no longer be chasing a downpayment that was going up faster with property appreciation than he could save. Given that this was new for the landlords and that their alternative was to share nothing and his alternative was to receive nothing, getting a 20% share was a great start.

This was making a lot of sense, and he could see how his equity would increase by tens of thousands of dollars over a short number of years just through inflation and his monthly equity contribution.

Kevin started to wonder if he could convince the couple that owned the home they were currently renting to consider this approach. Maybe if he made the investment more attractive for them using his approach, they would agree to give them a long-term agreement and find another home they could buy that would suit their needs when they had a baby.

*****

It was wishful thinking on Kevin's part. The Wilds weren't open to new ideas. They bought the home as an investment because they liked the neighbourhood. They didn't want to give up on the idea of living in it themselves.

Kevin decided to try out his idea with some other landlords who currently had rental ads posted online. After talking with a few people who were renting their investment properties out it seemed like they too questioned why they would give up a share. It was hard to get them to believe in the numbers when they only owned one property and didn't make investment decisions using sophisticated analysis on how to maximize their return over time while building a larger portfolio of homes.

Then Kevin thought about going to some of his business investor contacts who had passed on investing with him when he was funding the shotgun buyout.

After a few calls and a couple of in-person meetings with people on that list, he came away rejected and further disheartened. All those investors wanted to talk about was what had happened to his software company. It reminded him of how people gossip when someone they know dies and leaves a will that is contested by the family. It was insidious, like sharks circling potential prey waiting to see which one of them would take the first bite.

*****

After a particularly rough day at work, including the last lunch meeting he would take with a potential investor, Kevin flopped down on the couch in their rental house. Until he found some new inspiration there wasn't any point hearing more no's after repeating the same story.

He started to flip through movies to watch but wasn't paying close attention to the options as they scrolled by. He kept thinking over and over about how he needed to solve their problem of getting back to owning a home. It was the only way he could redeem himself in his own eyes and he believed it was also the only way to redeem himself in Jenny's eyes too.

As he continued flipping through his Netflix suggestions one thumbnail photo for a movie caught his eye. The face of a young Russell Crowe was staring back at him. The cover art for a movie called "A Beautiful Mind" was in the middle of the TV screen. It was like receiving a static electric shock as he remembered watching it the first time.

"Of course," Kevin said out loud, remembering the one famous scene that took place in the Princeton campus bar with a group of guys all trying to figure out how to pick up the blonde girl, though she only winked at John Nash (played by Russell Crowe). It was supposed to have given John Nash his truly original idea which was a better way to share rewards and reach agreements between multiple parties.

"What did he call it again?" Kevin thought as he hurriedly clicked play on the movie and sped up the playback to get to that pivotal part in the show.

"Right, the Nash Equilibrium," Kevin said in a drawn-out voice.

"That is it. This is exactly the proof I have been looking for that a better way to divide up the rewards in housing exists. John Nash's groundbreaking thesis from back in 1951." Kevin finished watching a bit more of the movie and then was too excited to stay seated on the couch. He went down to his computer and did some more research.

"Amazing," he said aloud after reading up on it all. New thoughts kept hitting Kevin's mind like successive cymbal crashes in a rock band's drum solo. "John Nash invented these tools for solving challenges with bargaining back in the early 50s and they are still rippling through the world in new ways after more than 70 years have passed. He deserved every part of the Nobel Prize he was awarded for coming up with his Equilibrium solution.

"Looking back on the pricing of homes in the '50s though, it is no wonder the need for a new model didn't exist back then. The average home value was only two times the average annual salary. Now, a family in any major city is lucky if just the downpayment isn't more than twice their annual salary."

Housing had become a media frenzy in the last few years. Kevin had his own personal experience with the challenges of housing now too. The media wasn't wrong in its assessment but journalists were grasping at straws for an answer to the problem. He wasn't even in as unfavourable a position as some families out there. "What if John Nash's work could help to solve housing finance problems also?" Kevin scribbled feverishly in his notebook trying to record all of the new ideas before they vanished from memory.

*****

After more time working on it, his new framework for applying a sharing model to the financial value of housing was starting to take shape. In looking at other businesses in the technology industry that Kevin was familiar with, there were examples like Airbnb, Uber, or ZipCar which were more well known companies considered part of the "sharing economy." Those companies created innovative ways to organize the use of assets like extra bedrooms or a vehicle through the use of software. Technology made the sharing more efficient and connected different parties to allow the sharing to occur. In the case of housing, it seemed like it was more a case of organizing capital in a new way. The funding was the challenge rather than the logistics of coordinating the parties involved since once someone moved in they would live there for many months.

Kevin worked on creating a package with everything he had learned including the forecast that showed the sharing results along with all of the income and expenses numbers based on the algorithm he'd built. He just needed to find the right person to present it to so he could get traction. He needed to show results from a small portfolio of homes to prove it worked. All of the investors he showed it to so far asked about the "track record." It was a common theme that people needed to see something to believe it.

*****

"The cleanup efforts are finally underway at the hospital," Jenny said, sounding upbeat. "And, the hospital foundation will be announcing a big new donation. The donor has agreed to contribute enough to upgrade all of the current surgical suites. Its got the staff smiling again for the first time since the fire."

"That's good to hear. What will that mean for patients who are treated there?" Kevin asked, wanting to hear more about what Jenny was working on, but also thinking back to his own experience waking up from a coma in that hospital.

"It means more advanced medical equipment, the latest laparoscopic surgical tools, less invasive surgeries that have faster recovery times and lower risks of complication or infection, and being able to offer procedures we couldn't provide before."

"That sounds incredible. It must be a very sizeable donation. Who's the donation being made by?" Kevin was curious about who would be that generous.

"Well it will be made public tomorrow at a press conference but his name is Paul Wright," Jenny said but also added not to tell anyone his name until after the press conference was done.

"I have heard of him. It's been a few years but I remember reading about him when he sold his company. He built an amazing business, and there was a long section of the article devoted to the things his staff said about working there. He created a zealous culture and his people absolutely loved that place."

Kevin remembered more about the details as he was talking.

He had to be a very intelligent guy too, Kevin was thinking. He remembered being very impressed by the company's industry-leading innovations.

"I think his company was in advanced automation and industrial controls if I remember correctly. It had many fortune 500 companies as customers. The company is still growing and successful today. The fact that it continues to grow years after his time at the helm ended is the mark of real leadership."

Suddenly taking in a deep breath, Kevin said to Jenny, "How could I get in touch with Paul? Can someone at the hospital introduce me?" Kevin was now thinking he could be the perfect person to work with on the new housing concept

"Let me see after tomorrow," Jenny replied with a hint of discomfort showing on her face.

What would Kevin call his concept though? He needed to name a new category so that it would be memorable if he was going to meet someone like Paul. How about something simple…

"Shared Equity Housing."

Kevin thought that could work. It needed to be about equity and not debt. Before the credit crisis, Kevin had heard advertising for mortgages that would fund more than 100% of the value of the home. Those mortgage products didn't work out too well for both the market and home buyers. The credit market did collapse from too much debt and in the end, the homeownership rate went down as a result.

"No, more debt isn't the answer," he thought, "this time, we need more equity."

*****

After reading all the media coverage of the hospital funding announcement, Kevin struggled to get a meeting with Paul through the hospital foundation's administrative contacts. Since Paul had made a big donation, Kevin worried that maybe Paul thought it was another request for charity since the introduction was coming through hospital staff. It did have the potential for a positive social impact, but Kevin believed it needed to stand on its own financially if it was going to scale up and become a business-based solution. There are too many people affected to think housing will be solved through donations.

The following week before heading into work, Kevin was surprised to see Doug at the coffee shop near his office. He hadn't seen Doug since the moment before he started his nearly deadly slide on their climbing trip. Doug was visibly embarrassed that he hadn't reached out to talk to him. He admitted it was very difficult to think of that day. He felt like he had gambled and came out on top while Kevin had been unlucky. If Kevin hadn't gone ahead while Doug was catching his breath it could have easily been him that fell but maybe he wouldn't have lived.

Kevin didn't feel like it was Doug's fault at all of course. It was his choice to go out in front and he could have been more careful by short roping with the rest of the guys rather than going unprotected. Anyway, he was happy to see him and the idea of going on another mountain climbing trip came to mind but he didn't bring it up. It would be like playing with fire to talk about with Jenny.

They chatted for a few more minutes and Kevin mentioned in passing the new shared equity housing concept he was working on. He didn't know why he decided to name drop but then told Doug he'd been trying to get a meeting with Paul Wright after hearing about the hospital endowment. Doug didn't react initially when he said it but as they were walking out, Doug threw his empty coffee cup in the bin and turned to look at Kevin and said, "I'll call Paul for you."

"What do you mean?" Kevin stopped and looked at Doug in the eyes.

"My older sister dated Paul for three years before he started his company and got so busy with it they decided to break up. He felt bad about it at the time realizing he couldn't ignore the opportunity but they stayed on good terms. If he doesn't remember me I am sure he would return my sister's call." Doug told Kevin that he would stay on it until Paul confirmed he would take a meeting.

"Well, I don't know what to say, Doug, thanks."

"Don't mention it." Doug said. "I can see what this means to you, and I want it to succeed." He shook Kevin's hand and nodded.

They went in separate directions but Kevin turned to stare at Doug while he got in his car and drove off. Shaking his head he thought, "It is so strange how all the twists and turns in our lives work out with the benefit of hindsight. Now I need to get ready." Kevin knew that Doug wouldn't stop until he had his meeting with Paul, and Kevin wasn't going to waste the opportunity.

Chapter 6
WITH A GREAT VIEW

Walking into Paul's office, on the top floor of the tallest office building in town, made a jaw-dropping first impression on Kevin. After selling his company Paul had leased a small but stunning space in the city's most recently constructed office tower which gave him an incredible view out over everything. Looking out the windows from the waiting area by the reception desk presented Kevin with a view of tens of thousands of homes. Most of the west half of the city was visible between where he was standing and the horizon. It was like he was standing on the precipice of both a problem and an opportunity. All that real estate spread out in front of him in need of new funding options. This view was a breathtaking backdrop for what he was about to present to Paul.

When Kevin finally got to meet Paul he could see that he deserved his reputation. He was incredibly personable, a "salt of the earth kinda person." Kevin immediately felt comfortable with him and knew right away he was exactly the kind of business person he would like to partner with.

Paul was an engineer by training so he was very comfortable working through numbers and diving into Kevin's projections. Paul had even hired two people he referred to as "quants," who he explained came from a background in graduate physics and mathematics but had migrated into financial analysis to work in the investment industry. They joined his small team to help Paul pick investments that would out-perform the market. He never stopped looking for better ways to productively invest the capital he had from the sale of his company. He always liked to have them come into meetings about new ideas to hear feedback from their point of view.

Before they dove into the presentation Kevin had prepared, Paul wanted to ask Kevin about his software company and what had happened. Unlike the other vulture capital investors that Kevin had endured questioning him before, Paul had a distinctly different tone. He related his own experience with Kevin's and somehow guessed a number of the events that took place. Paul was a very shrewd businessman and had a tremendous network of contacts throughout the city. He had gathered more intel than anyone else Kevin had met with to gain some insight into what happened with Kevin's old software company. Paul then told Kevin a story of one of his early business experiences before calling for the quants to come into the room. Paul described getting into business with a partner who also tried to buy him out with a shotgun clause. In the end Paul wasn't able to come up with the money. However, he took the proceeds he walked away with and his desire to prove his ex-business partner wrong, and went on to build the success story he became most well known for.

All that Kevin could do was sit back in his chair in quiet acknowledgement of how fortunate he was to meet with someone like Paul. "What an amazing guy," he thought to himself. With Paul's display of generosity towards the hospital, Kevin considered that Paul may be motivated by the potential positive social impact the housing program would have for families. Rather than starting on that note, Kevin decided to base his pitch for Shared Equity Housing on its financial merits first. He figured that with Paul being a business-minded investor and one who probably followed Harvard Business school professor Michael Porter's philosophy on "shared value[1]," he would want to know that it would be a financially sustainable enterprise rather than a project that depended on charity to solve all the world's problems.

Kevin started into the discussion on his Shared Equity concept. "All large-scale innovation in housing finance throughout the last 100 years has centred around mortgages and banking institutions. Innovations that included the creation of the central banks, to the housing associations that provide loan insurance, and to the invention and evolution of mortgage-backed securities. All the work finance professionals have done which achieved major milestones in the improvement of home financing sources, was all based entirely on debt."

"Now, and for the future, the new focus needs to be on equity." Kevin could hear the conviction in his own voice.

"In the months leading up to the credit crisis, borrowers had seemingly unlimited access to debt, yet the homeownership rate only inched up by 2%[2]."

"And what did all that debt do? It destabilized the housing market and resulted in the biggest wave of foreclosures ever recorded[3]. In the end it left us with a lower level of homeownership than at any time in the prior 15 years." Kevin was on a roll.

He continued through his presentation, weaving in the story of re-discovering the movie with Russell Crowe about Nobel laureate John Nash[4].

Then he presented the savings in ownership costs achievable by holding real estate with a shared equity contract compared to regular property management. He had all of the numbers broken down with several timely examples from publicly disclosed financial statements.

He showed that banks on average pay 1/10th the cost[5] for administering their mortgage asset compared to the combined costs of property management, maintenance and vacancy that a landlord would have renting the very same house.

No Property Manager Hassles   **No Maintenance Expenses**   **No Vacancy Costs**

By eliminating those costs for the investor, by having the tenant look after the home as any owner would, and then by adding the tenant's monthly equity savings on top, the investor came out ahead even after sharing 20% of the equity growth.

In fact, the benefit to the investor can be 2.5 times the cost of sharing 20% of the growth in equity. All of that is achieved by cutting down on three areas of cost: management, maintenance and vacancy[6].

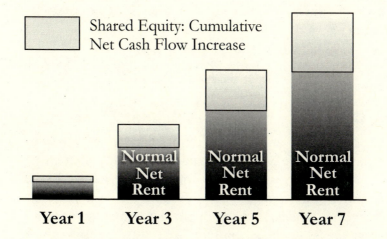

The key outcome for the investor was a better financial return with less time spent managing the investment, all because the tenant's interests were now aligned with the investor's. This alignment dramatically decreases the time required to manage a portfolio of homes compared to regular residential rental assets. The improved cash flow with a shared equity agreement enables investment in higher quality homes in better locations, which have the potential to grow in value faster on average than lower quality older housing stock[7].

Paul then asked about what it looked like from the tenant's perspective. Kevin showed Paul a projection of how the tenant's equity grew, which made Paul's eyes open wider. As the tenant contributed towards their equity savings, and shared in the growth in value, their equity grew at a staggering speed. With the monthly savings contribution and the share in the home's growth in the value, the tenant now had skin the game. They had something to avoid losing as well as something to gain by the home being properly maintained.

Kevin then thought of a new way to position the situation for tenants that he had never thought of before.

"What if the tenant's share was not based on them successfully buying the home. What if the tenant built up equity and received their share so long as they looked after the home and paid their monthly payments on time. Then when the home is sold based on the tenant being ready to move out, they would get their share the same as if they bought the home themselves." Kevin was tingling, thinking that was the difference that mattered. That was the final missing piece that changed the game for tenants and landlords.

"All of the old fashioned rent-to-own programs that have been tried before, resulted in the tenant losing all their equity if they did't buy. But Shared Equity Housing isn't rent-to-own. It is a simple equitable share of the growth in value." Kevin kept going with his train of thought.

"The number one measurement of success is that both parties grow their equity in the home. People's lives change from one year to the next so we will always be ready to sell the home if the tenant needs to move after a few years, but in that case, they still share in the equity growth." Kevin was nearly finished but thought of a way to appeal to Paul's better nature.

"Besides, nobody wants to be the bad guy. The people we do business with don't want to knowingly enter into an agreement which incentivizes them to cheat. Tenants certainly don't want to lose their equity to the landlord. I also believe that people won't en masse enter into an investment they know is designed to take advantage of someone. Shared Equity is the solution and does away with the old rent-to-own agreements of the past. The tenant's share is realized even if they don't take title to the home themselves."

Kevin ended on a strong note and filled his chest up with a big breath, satisfied he had delivered a compelling presentation.

Paul was nodding along while the two quants sitting next to Paul had quizzical looks on their faces. Kevin's read of their expression was that they were interested to do more analysis themselves but hadn't immediately negated everything he had just presented like many of the other investors had.

Kevin let the message sink in while they were all silently thinking to themselves, staring out the expansive windows of the meeting room on the penthouse floor. Kevin started to visualize how Paul's standing would grow further by being the champion for a new housing program that could be spread across the country. This could be the true starting point for Shared Equity Housing.

Paul turned to Kevin after a pause, and with a warm smile said, "Kevin, thank you for coming to explain this new concept. It's a fascinating combination of ideas. As with anything we see, we will do our research and run our own projections but I think it's safe to say we are intrigued."

"That's wonderful to hear Paul, thank you for your willingness to listen and your time so far," Kevin finished.

He didn't expect to get a yes answer on the spot but couldn't help himself and asked when a good time to follow up would be. Paul said two weeks and Kevin thanked him again before heading out to go down in the elevator.

*****

Four days later Paul's name came up on Kevin's phone as it started to ring.

"That's funny, sooner than I expected," Kevin thought.

"Hello Kevin," Paul said, "what would we start with as the first step for your Shared Equity Housing concept? How would we begin?" Paul asked.

"That is a great question. First, we can start with one home where my family will be the guinea pig. Once the first one is done and we have a final set of all of the required documents then we complete nine more to round out the initial portfolio to ten. After a year of operating those ten, we can then look to expand from there with the experience and the additional refined knowledge we gather along the way." Kevin had already thoroughly mapped out the steps to begin ramping up the program.

"Okay. You got it," Paul said.

"Ah, what do you mean?" Kevin was taken by surprise.

"Let's start with the first one to get the documents finished then complete nine more. Clark at our office will organize it all with you and coordinate the paperwork. I am looking forward to seeing how much we can expand the pie." Paul had agreed to fund the first portfolio to operate the program and was referring to the entrepreneurial idea that innovative products create more value for everyone and enlarge the economic pie.

"That sounds great! I am looking forward to working with you and your team." Kevin's excitement was bubbling over so he wanted to finish the call and hang up before his luck ran out. This was far more satisfying than the day he had confirmed the final amount needed for the shotgun buyout. This felt somehow more permanent and lasting.

*****

Kevin couldn't wait to tell Jenny. He sent her a text message right away.

"Paul is backing the housing program!"

"Really? What does that mean?" Jenny texted back.

"We get to be the first family to do it. We get to look at moving into a house now where we will have a long-term agreement." Kevin typed. "Then I will go out and work with nine more families to do the same thing."

"Moving again?" was Jenny's reply.

"Maybe not. Going to call the couple to see if they will sell us our rental."

"I doubt it." Jenny replied.

Kevin remained optimistic: "We will see :)"

*****

Kevin called the landlords that night and asked them if they would look at an offer to sell their home? He said he and a partner were looking to buy. The couple said they still wanted to move into it eventually but would think about it overnight. They called back the next day to confirm that they weren't interested in selling it. "Well, Jenny was right," Kevin thought.

It was time to go house hunting. This time though, they were in the driver's seat.

Jenny wasn't looking forward to upsetting the kids' schedule again but she was happier they wouldn't have to worry about being forced to leave on short notice. She was unsure about parts of it because she didn't know Paul well. But then she told Kevin that she realized they were going to be forced to move at some point so better to do it when they could control the timing.

While looking at homes for sale in neighbourhoods that could work for them they considered buying a newly built home. Kevin was surprised that he hadn't already thought to approach home builders about his Shared Equity concept. He made a note of that to come back to later.

After finding two homes that would work and touring through them they failed to get an accepted offer on anything because the condition period Paul's team wanted to complete their due diligence was too long. The sellers just wouldn't agree to have their homes tied up and off the market for over a month. Kevin debated the buying process with them to find an approach that could work.

They were starting to worry that they wouldn't find a home. The next day an automatic alert popped up in Jenny's email, triggered by the preferences she had entered online to filter through all homes that came on the market. It was a little farther from the kids' school but it could work. Jenny's big priority was to have stability again, and this seemed like the opportunity to do that. It was a solid respectable nondescript family home.

As luck would have it, the week before they removed conditions on the house they were purchasing as a Shared Equity home with Paul, they got word from Frank and Louise Wild, letting them know they were expecting a baby. A week later Kevin had a big grin on his face when he was able to give their official notice that they would be ending their tenancy agreement and moving out of the rental. He was looking forward to growing their equity again and no longer having an axe suspended above their necks.

*****

Moving into their new shared equity home was much less of a hassle than they had feared. After their prior move into the rental house they had simplified their lives by getting rid of stuff they no longer had room for. It was much easier to transfer everything over to the next home. Compared to how draining it was before to leave their dream home, knowing they were building towards something in the future gave them a boost of positive energy.

Rob came by to visit them in the new place and to hear more about the shared equity concept. Kevin recently couldn't stop himself from telling everyone about it. Rob being there to visit begged the question of whether another mountain climbing trip was in the cards too. In all of the years they had been climbing, they had never seen another person suffer the kind of fall Kevin had when they were roped up. It made Kevin think that maybe he could learn how to get back up on the horse and control his fear. He knew that no matter what, they would never go up anything with exposure again without fully protecting themselves. Any time that a risk could be mitigated, he would never again rationalize taking that risk for the sake of expediency. They simply needed to plan enough time into the schedule to always be methodical.

Rob could think of three different peaks that were easier than what they had climbed in the past. He was thinking of a mountain that would be great exercise but not leave them gripped out of their minds with exposure and risk. It would be great to have the four of them back together on an adventure again. Kevin liked the idea of reconnecting with Doug too after he had doggedly persisted to get the meeting confirmed with Paul. That meeting led to his family getting a new home.

Kevin was feeling conflicted about it, but then he started looking forward to going on another mountain adventure.

*****

With the move into the new home done, Kevin decided to plan out a whole romantic evening with Jenny to celebrate. Jenny was looking forward to a night out to have some great food and a glass of her favourite wine. It took some time getting back into the groove because it had been too long since their last real date night. With the tension of the hospital fire, and the volatility of work and issues with the house before that, it was hard to call any of the other times they went out for dinner a "date" since Kevin had started his current job. Those evenings felt more like just eating food rather than time to connect again.

He made a reservation at the Fig Tree Bistro. He hadn't been back since the day the shotgun clause had been triggered, which now seemed like the trigger for all the chaos that had followed. He wanted to create a good memory there, one that would mark the start of their future plans. Looking at Jenny across the table, he hoped they could put their misfortune behind them and build the life they wanted. He hoped Jenny still wanted the same.

"The last time I was here was the day everything began to go wrong," he told her. "I'm hoping this is the day everything starts to go right."

Jenny nodded. "I hope so," she said. Kevin was thinking that she still seemed hesitant to hope for too much, still seemed unwilling to count on anything that wasn't tangible.

But then she reached across the table and took his hand. "I really do," she said.

It was a small gesture, but it seemed like Jenny had opened a door — not much, but enough. Kevin wondered for a moment whether to take the chance and step into that opening, or to accept it as a beginning and wait for her to open up more.

He decided not to hold back.

"Jenny, I know how hard this has been, on you, on all of us. But I feel like I've got some real momentum now, that I can launch something that will work for us, and for other families too." He told her not just about the Shared Equity plans themselves, but about everything he hoped it could be, about what he hoped it would mean for the two of them and for their family.

And then Jenny was telling him about all that she had feared but hadn't wanted to mention, but that she was starting to sense the momentum, too. Kevin felt like the door between them was opening, they were talking the way they used to.

The food was delicious and they ended up ordering a bottle of wine after having a glass each so they decided to summon a car to take them home.

When they sat down in the rear seat, their hands naturally came together as they laid their heads back onto the head rests, staring straight up at the roof of the car. Kevin loosened the top of his shirt and breathed out in a sigh of satisfaction for the great night as all of the muscles in his body relaxed and he sunk into the leather seat cushion.

Not even thinking, Kevin leaned over and kissed Jenny, reminded again about how great she looked. Jenny reached up to hold the edge of his jaw as he did. The kiss continued on, and Jenny stretched her outside leg over the top of Kevin's knee that was closest to her. This was getting exciting. Kevin was taken back in time to the first year after they met when they tried to stop at a lookout point on a deserted highway in the summer one night when the stars were out. They had gotten so caught up in the moment that they had taken off most of their clothes right before a patrol car happened to drive by. They had to quickly turn on the ignition and drive away but only had enough time to throw their shirts back on. When the patrol car passed them going the other direction, after pulling a U-turn to come and check on why their car was stopped, everything looked normal, but they were still naked from the waist down.

Making out in the back seat of the car that was driving them home, brought back memories of all the hot-blooded youthful years in their relationship, before they knew about the cut-throat business world or the hard lessons life had in store for them.

When they got home they said an expedited goodbye to the babysitter and Kevin teased that he was going to chase Jenny into the bedroom. Now they were having fun.

While Jenny was trying to get her dress off to hang it, Kevin, who had stripped down to his underwear right away, stood behind her and started to nibble on her neck while putting his hands on both of her breasts. She tried, unsuccessfully, to get her dress up on the hangar while he was touching the tips of his fingers to the most sensitive spots. Then as she was trying one last time to get the dress hung up, Kevin moved a hand down to the bottom of the triangle on the front of her panties and she dropped the dress to turn around and kiss him hard on the mouth. She leaned against him to walk him back towards the bed and pushed. He fell back onto the bed and then she seductively crawled up on top.

Kevin was in ecstasy. Jennifer arched her back and moved with him and had her hands on his chest. She then leaned down to wrap her arms around the back of his neck.

"Let's have another baby Kevin," Jenny whispered into his ear between heavy breaths. "I want to get pregnant again." Jenny seemed electrified from head to toe. Every one of Kevin's nerve endings was lit up as he edged closer to complete overload. She began to slow down and closed her eyes tightly, desperately absorbed in the moment. Kevin was nearly there himself so he pressed his body harder. He liked it when they shared the final moment of ecstasy at the same time. Then they both let themselves go.

Releasing one another they rolled out on the bed, facing each other on their sides, still panting.

"Are you sure you want to have another kid now?" Kevin said, trying not to sound incredulous.

"Yes. Yes, of course I do," Jenny said. "What's changed since we were trying before?" Now it was her turn to be incredulous.

"That was two years ago and now we are just in a different place. Mella and Danny are older. It feels like we have moved on to the next chapter in our lives," Kevin said.

"Why didn't you bring this up before?" Jenny was now getting frustrated.

"I just thought it would be better to leave the issue for you to raise when you were ready. I wasn't even sure you wanted to try again after what happened last time." Kevin thought he was making sense. Jenny became more tense in response.

"So are you saying no then?" Jenny asked him pointedly.

"Let me think. It's a bit out of the blue and I honestly thought it was in the past," Kevin said.

Jenny got up off the bed and went to the bathroom

Kevin could hear her opening and closing drawers and turning the faucet on and off with hard distinct movements.

*****

They would talk about having another baby three more times in the following two weeks. The more they talked about it the more animosity built up. Kevin was becoming certain it wasn't something that would work for them. He couldn't see it being an improvement for their two kids' lives. They already had more than enough ways to expend their parenting energy with Daniel and especially with Mella.

The more that Kevin rationalized why he didn't want to have another child, the more Jenny became adamant that she did. Jennifer's mother and father each had two other siblings and she had many memories of seeing her parents visiting with their brothers and sisters over the holidays. Those were some of the happiest experiences she remembered having with her parents while she was growing up.

She never had a brother or sister because after she was born her mother had developed some cysts which at the time were usually treated with a hysterectomy. Now it was possible with laparoscopic surgery to avoid a hysterectomy which might have allowed her mother to get pregnant again. Jenny found out about what happened to her mother when she was 17 after a particularly joyous holiday with extended family. She had asked her mom why she didn't have more kids and was finally old enough to hear her mom's tearful story. Her mom's story had made her want to have three kids of her own. It was also a big reason why she got into health care. She continued to work relentlessly at shifting wasted resources over into improving the hospital's surgical capabilities.

Jenny had talked about some of these experiences with Kevin. Her view of what their family could be and his belief about what they already had were simply opposed. They couldn't know which decision would turn out better in the future. They only had their opinions. The friction resulting from the opposition over having another baby began to erode the positive connection they had re-established after moving into the new home. Resolution wasn't anywhere in sight.

*****

Rob Wells called on a Saturday morning to say that the other guys were confirmed for their next mountain adventure. He left it open, not assuming Kevin was automatically going to decide to come with them. Since seeing Rob at their house a few weeks earlier and without Rob knowing it, Kevin had all but committed in his mind to go on the next trip. Not remembering that Jenny had no idea he was planning to go on another climb, he casually mentioned the date the group had scheduled as if she would take that to mean he was going to be gone for that weekend too.

Jenny was seething when he clarified that he was also thinking of going with them. She was on the edge of exploding, fuelled by one part rage and one part fear over what might happen.

"You are being reckless! How can you even bring yourself to go out again with those guys?" Jenny was nearly screaming.

"What happened before wasn't any of their faults, and they saved me by getting me out," Kevin pleaded, but could see that it wasn't anywhere close to the real issue that was eating away at her. "We are going up a much easier mountain. Most people that go up it wouldn't describe it as climbing. It's just a long hike." He continued to try to allay her concerns.

Their debate lasted a little longer but Kevin could see there was nothing he could say to change her mind. He stopped arguing and went to assist Mella with her school project, trying to deescalate the argument while doing something to help their daughter.

The trouble was, he knew he wanted to go.

Jenny would be fine when they all came back safe, he thought.

He hoped.

*****

The route they chose to climb was an easy and straightforward approach up the mountain. There was supposed to be a small amount of glacier travel from the middle to near the three-quarter mark on the way up, but it was a low-angle slope with no sign of any cracks or weaknesses. No matter what, on this trip, they agreed they were going to be roped up whenever there was even a chance of exposure, and practice proper communication while moving. Any worry of misreading a hidden crevasse, loose rock, or potential for extended slide meant they would stay secured to each other.

They were already having a great time on the trip. It was just like when they were in their early twenties. Telling stories, heckling each other, and enjoying the best freeze-dried meals on the market.

Gerry had been eating like a vegetarian over prior months and realized as they were cooking their evening meal that almost all of the food packages the other three had brought contained some sort of meat combination.

"Did this group bring up even a single food package that isn't stuffed with meat?" Gerry remarked.

"Well if there is let's get rid of it," Doug quipped.

"What would I do without you guys," Gerry sneered back.

Rob unveiled a small flask of whiskey he'd brought which contained what he called "mountain proof." They each had a swig to warm their throats and calm their nerves before crawling into the tents before sunset. As usual they would be waking up early for summit day on Saturday.

It was overcast in the hours before dawn but Kevin felt calm and collected. This was going to be a whole new experience getting up to the top of the mountain. They put on their crampons and roped up when they hit the frozen snow. Their pace was measured, their handling of rope and anchoring gear where needed was disciplined. Luckily the clouds drifted away when they were two hours from the top of the mountain. They all started to feel like they were entering a new chapter of their lives with that day representing the opening page.

Kevin had changed. He was so much more patient than when they had been out with him before. The angst and the edginess to his ego were gone. He was more deliberate in everything he did. The adrenaline from the climb wasn't brewing just beneath the surface of his composure like it had been in the past. He was always breathing fully, in complete control of his headspace.

Kevin could feel a difference himself. He was acutely aware of the stress response his body could produce and how to calm himself back down with attention to his stomach muscles and diaphragm. With concentrated relaxation, he found he could make better decisions even when others were anxious around him. Having gained some distance from his past struggles, he now knew how to find clarity in a situation and think straight even in the most chaotic circumstances.

Moving for five hours without incident, ascending up the remaining ridge towards the bottom of the snow gullies, and then up to where the edge of the snowfield transitioned into the final section of frozen glacier, they were in sight of the last stretch leading to the summit cone. With about 90 minutes left to go before they hit the summit, Gerry started to struggle with fatigue. Although it wasn't as steep, the elevation on this peak was greater than the mountain they had attempted to climb last. The reduced oxygen was starting to affect them even though the climbing wasn't at all technical. Gerry seemed to be affected more than the other three to the point where he became truly exhausted. Kevin was second from the front in the group of four and Gerry was right behind him so Kevin could tell that he was tired by how much he was lagging back on the rope.

"Let's take a food break," Kevin called out loud enough for Rob in front of him and Gerry and Doug behind him to hear.

"Sure." "Yup." "Good call." Kevin heard in response. The four of them stopped moving as they bunched closer together so they could chat while they rested.

"How are you doing Gerry?" Kevin asked.

"I don't know man. I am drained. More than I can remember being on any mountain before." Gerry's chest was heaving while he worked up the poise to give his reply. Kevin stared off into the distance for a moment before responding.

"I have an idea," Kevin said. "I remember reading about the principle of 'equal-suffering' in an article on building teams. The idea is that if everyone is working at the same relative level of effort then everyone will reach the end goal equally tired, but reach it successfully together."

"Okay. So what?" Rob said.

"If Gerry is more tired than the rest of us right now, that means he is putting in more effort, relatively speaking. We need to balance it out so it's just as tough for the rest of us. What we do is take all the weight he's carrying plus the backpack itself and distribute amongst us. Then we'll all have to put in more effort to match him."

Being that they were all competitive athletes in their younger days, they had no hesitation accepting the challenge. Now it became about who could suffer more than Gerry. They relished the idea of testing their endurance again.

It was somehow more satisfying to arrive at the summit that day, mutually wrecked.

"Woa-yeah!" Rob shouted first as he crested the edge to the small plateau on the summit.

"Who-rah!" "Holy Shit!" Kevin and Doug managed to yell out as they caught up with Rob. Gerry held up his fist in the air in a victorious pose but was gasping to catch his breath and didn't have the strength to call out. They were all in a state of whimpering exhaustion but arriving at the summit melted away all remaining tension they were carrying.

They all dropped into a seated position at the same time, half breathing half coughing with satisfaction.

The clouds had fully retreated over the mountain to the east and the sun was high in the sky. It turned out to be a gorgeous day. The group of four sat there peacefully taking in the expansive panorama laid out between them and the azure blue horizon. Some wispy cloud remains hung above a lower mountain nearby, drifting aimlessly over the ridge-top. The sunlight was reflecting off the mirror like surface of a valley lake off in the distance. The glow from the water's surface was a laser line of orange light leading from below the location of the sun straight towards their vantage point.

Kevin felt his endorphins kick in. It was warm at the top and with a moment of stillness, his blood absorbed enough oxygen for his mental sharpness to return. Sitting on that pinnacle provided an aspect of the plane between all earthly objects and the domed atmosphere above. It was like his consciousness lifted above his body giving him perspective on himself and what he had worked towards over the years.

Kevin started to focus on how much time he still had left. Even after all he had done in his life, there were decades left to experience. He could plan to spend a couple of decades doing something that really mattered and he would still have many years beyond that to enjoy his time on this spectacular planet.

"What path would be worth travelling for 20 years straight, if we knew that's how long it would take?" Kevin spoke aloud, not expecting an answer from any of them. Looking out into the open expanse before him, he knew it was the question he needed to answer for himself.

Chapter 7
APART

Their equity was already growing by Kevin's calculations. He found a website that published a simple index of home values in his region and over the first three months of living in the home, values had gone up 1.2%. With their share of the mortgage pay-down, the share of the appreciation, and the savings contributions they made every month their equity had already gone up by thousands. That was the power of Shared Equity Housing. Of course it also meant that Paul's equity had gone up by even more because the investor shared 20% and held onto 80% of the increase in equity value.

He had already helped two other families get into homes and had five more families just starting to tour houses to see what they liked. At this pace, they would complete the funding for the last of the 10 homes for the initial test portfolio within seven months of launching. The families would put up a deposit that amounted to three to four months' rent and then contribute anywhere between $250-$375 per month towards their own equity once they had moved in. Kevin experienced a learning curve in figuring out how to describe it to people who saw the ad he'd been running. Once a potential Shared Equity buyer saw the equity growth numbers from their share in property appreciation and mortgage pay down they would immediately become visibly excited. It was like a spark of hope appeared in front of them as the futility of their past efforts towards homeownership was forgotten.

When he arrived home from the mountain trip, Kevin was weary but full from the sensory feast he had just devoured. He could see, however, that Jenny was unnerved from waiting at home all weekend. She was restless from wondering if he would *walk* through the door Sunday night or require some other means of transportation to be delivered back to the city.

Kevin had known he had to go on the trip. He felt fulfilled from getting to the summit in a way he hadn't when he was younger. That irresistible magnetic force of the mountain calling him back was starting to dissipate though. The new frame of mind he discovered on the summit was profound, and he planned to ask the question over and over until he found a satisfying answer. *What could he do that might take at least 20 years but would be worth such an investment of time?*

*****

The mountain trip invigorated Kevin enough to approach Paul about expanding the scope of their investment plan to encompass more homes. He also remembered needing to meet with some of the larger home builders in the city to find out how Shared Equity Housing could work for them. He hoped it could help them sell their homes faster. If there were a large enough population of people in the city who would move into a home because they would be working towards homeownership, it could be an untapped market for builders. The home builders could then finish their projects faster and grow their businesses.

He thought it might present a problem for them if they needed to get the money out of each home as it sold to start building the next one in their subdivision or start another project. That would take some more planning and thinking to figure out.

Jenny's work was absorbing more of her time than in the past. She was rising up the management ladder at the hospital and spent some evenings throughout the week in their den at home still engaged with issues from the hospital. They both had their heads down with their jobs and their two kids. Jennifer's team at the hospital had finished planning the upgrades to the operating theatre. The funds pledged by Paul for the hospital foundation had been received and for a few weeks both she and Kevin were sending reports to the same people at Paul's office. They were both grateful for the impact Paul's decisions had made in their respective lives.

As Jenny was finishing the work following Paul's donation, Kevin was looking to increase the investment into Shared Equity Housing. Kevin believed it was time to meet with Paul again in person. Although after talking with Paul, who was supportive of doing more, Kevin realized there would inevitably be a limit to how many of these homes Paul could fund. Housing consumed a lot of capital very quickly and given the nature of real estate it couldn't be immediately sold like stocks or bonds. Paul would only ever hold a part of his portfolio in real estate assets so Kevin needed to start looking for other ways of expanding the funding sources for Shared Equity Housing. The people who moved into the first homes gave him such positive feedback that he wanted to keep going and accommodate many more families.

Kevin was finding it enjoyable on the weekends to work with the people who responded to his ads to help them understand how they could use the Shared Equity approach to become homeowners. Looking at how many people didn't own a home, there were millions of people across the country who could improve their equity position using the sharing program. However, It had taken a lot of time to get the funding just to set up 10 families with homes. How could he ever grow enough to open up the opportunity to thousands — let alone millions of people?

During Kevin's meeting at Paul's office, the "quant" guys talked about a particular stock they owned which he said held large-scale income-producing real estate assets. Since they had spent time investigating it before buying shares they had gotten to know some of the management team at the company. They passed along the contact information to Kevin for one of the people they had met who was an acquisition manager for the fund. Looking at the contact info Kevin saw the company's name was Cathedral REIT. They told Kevin that REIT stands for Real Estate Investment Trust which is the name for a preferred legal vehicle used for holding income-producing real estate when the fund is traded on a stock exchange. Apparently, it was better for tax purposes. Cathedral REIT happened to be one of the largest owners of rental apartments and had its head office located in their city.

If Kevin was going to find a way to make homeownership possible for millions more, talking with the Cathedral people would be a good place to start. Maybe he could convince them to create a new division for Shared Equity Housing? Kevin called to set up the meeting with the executive who was happy to discuss a new idea. "Great," he thought, "seems easy enough."

*****

The day of his appointment to meet with the manager of acquisitions for Cathedral REIT, the sky was clouded over and cold. It wasn't raining but the clouds seemed very close to the ground and they screened the sunlight, making the day dark and dreary. The meeting was scheduled at the Cathedral's office.

As Kevin walked through the front doors he stopped momentarily to look up. Entering the office building was like walking into the galactic empire's headquarters. The REIT occupied the entire building and the entrance lobby made any visitor feel small and inconsequential. The whole foyer was dark obsidian and charcoal granite polished to the sheen of a soldier's shoes on parade day. The guard desk had two or three people queued up at any one time waiting for their picture to be taken so small ID stickers could be printed. There were no plants or anything green but there was a large sculpture that looked like an abstract collection of oblong shapes welded together, fashioned out of a coppery-brass coloured metal. There were three very large mural canvasses hung on the primary wall behind and above the guard desk stretching to within inches of the ceiling. The combined painting shown on the set of three was hard to describe. It looked like a maelstrom of deep red and orange with streaks of dark black tar-like paint in a vortex shape at the centre of the middle canvass. Each of them had to be at least six feet wide and well over 25 feet tall.

After interacting with the subtly rude attendant from the third-party security service, Kevin took his ID and scanned through the turnstile heading for the elevator. Putting his ID sticker on his jacket lapel felt too much like bowing down in servitude so he kept it in his hand on top of his notebook.

Arriving on the reception floor one level from the top of the building, the waiting area stretched fully around one-quarter of the floor. It was a wide open lounge with multiple banks of designer leather couches. They were more for looks than comfort it seemed. After confirming with the receptionist who he was there to meet with, he sat down to find the couch quite hard and unforgiving.

Five minutes later, Andrew Brock came out to meet Kevin. Andrew handed him his card, which stated that his title was VP of Acquisitions. Andrew led Kevin into one of the meeting rooms that looked out towards the park across the street. Kevin always kept his back to the windows in meeting rooms like this. Taking in the streetscape for a moment Kevin sat down on the correct chair so he wouldn't have the outside light in his eyes. They started the discussion in earnest following the standard pleasantries and Kevin went through a similar presentation to the one he gave Paul. Rather than a warm responsive interaction, Andrew simply nodded, showing little emotion.

Andrew seemed to be a likeable guy. He didn't have any questions for Kevin about the program which Kevin thought odd. Andrew went on to tell Kevin more about how strong Cathedral was and that they could use their balance sheet and publicly traded stock to fund homes at a lower cost than any other real estate owner out there. Andrew believed their size would allow them to convince the banks to provide Cathedral lower interest rates on the mortgages they would normally use for funding part of the cost of the homes. This all sounded great until Andrew described their process for looking at real estate acquisitions.

Andrew finished the conversation by explaining that being the VP of acquisitions, he would need to sit down with the chief investment officer and if she found it worth considering, she would take it to the CEO and CFO along with the rest of the investment committee for further discussion. For Cathedral's process they didn't look at anything new in the quarter it was presented. They only worked off of the stated strategic plan for the year that was approved by the full board of directors at the prior year-end meeting. The plan could be adjusted each quarter after a normal scheduled board meeting but with something unique like the Shared Equity Housing program it could take a full calendar year to appear in the strategic plan. Once it was formally adopted into the plan then they could begin looking at assets to acquire.

"It can take persistence to start anything new," Andrew summarized. "Most people we talk to aren't stubborn enough."

"Well, I'm exactly that stubborn," Kevin said with a wide grin.

"Looks like I'm gonna be in this for the long haul," Kevin thought. After a diplomatic goodbye, Kevin walked out of the office building and saw the clouds were starting to thin out making it brighter outside. He vowed to keep following up with them and even explore the idea with some other large real estate groups.

Realistically though, it was probably going to take years.

On the other hand, strangely, Kevin hadn't seen anything else out there that had the potential to safely increase homeownership like the Shared Equity approach. He decided it didn't matter if it was slow going, no one else seemed to be doing anything new that was working in a big way so if this was the only option then it was worth pursuing for as long as it took to become successful.

*****

That Thursday night they had a big gala event to attend. Through Paul's network, Jenny and Kevin had been invited to the city's biggest annual fundraising event which was organized for the local cancer foundation. It typically attracted the highest-profile VIPs and was an incredibly well-attended event. There would be over a thousand people there and the ticket prices were not insubstantial. The event had raised over eight million dollars last year and was already expected to surpass that with the donations they were receiving leading up to it.

The main ballroom within the conference centre was a sight to behold. There was a screen on stage that stretched one-third of the width of the room and had different stylized images slowly appearing in different places as people walked in. The lighting and audio equipment set up was to the level of a concert and the tables were elegantly dressed with a bouquet arrangement in the middle that tastefully included the cancer foundation's logo.

The whole evening was like a movie premiere with the way guests were dressed. The suits and gowns and jewelry were stunning. Kevin had on a classic black suit and white shirt with a black bow tie. Jenny had on her favourite outfit which was a sage coloured full length double layer satin dress with a low cut cowl neck. She also had on a pearl necklace with matching earrings and her favourite shade of lipstick. She looked stunning.

The event saw two different musical groups perform during the evening. One was professional but the opening act was a local high school jazz band. Not expecting too much of them Kevin was in awe over how good they were. Thinking that he would hear some poorly done outdated jazz songs, the audience was blown away with their musical acumen when they performed big band cover versions of current hit songs.

The group sitting at Jenny and Kevin's table had broken the ice as soon as they sat down and were a talkative bunch. As people got to know each other, Valerie Gagne, a woman sitting next to Kevin, turned out to be a long-time donor to the cancer foundation and was a friend of Paul's. Kevin shared his background and how he came to meet Paul following the endowment announcement for the hospital. He introduced Valerie to Jenny too and mentioned how she also knew Paul through being the one that looked after the planning process for the new surgical suites.

Valerie described her experience with the cancer foundation and how she had known the executive director for a long time. Valerie drew a parallel with how Kevin was essentially trying to raise capital for housing. She told Kevin the story about how the foundation learned to increase their fundraising results.

"They found the voice of hope," she said. "If they told everyone how many people died while receiving financial support through the funding the foundation obtained, their fundraising results would be destroyed." She added, "They had to keep the message of hope front and centre to inspire people to contribute to the goal of beating cancer. People have to hear personal stories of all of those families who have fought and survived with the help of the foundation. There will always be a risk and always be hurdles to overcome. When people see the miraculous effects their involvement could have, they can overcome the mind's natural protective instinct and come to wholeheartedly believe in the cause. That's how they've brought together the people you see here before you tonight." Her voice raised in fervour at the end and she made a grand sweeping gesture out with her arms.

"What an inspiring woman," Kevin thought. He would remember to mention her name to Paul when he saw him next.

"I should see if Valerie wants to join the hospital foundation's board. We need someone with her passion in that group," Jenny whispered into Kevin's ear.

The fundraising gala event went on to break prior years' records and would be talked about for weeks following. Everyone in attendance felt imbued with uplifting energy that reverberated throughout the hall from the music and especially the closing remarks.

*****

Saturday morning Kevin woke up enlivened to figure out a new plan for the Shared Equity Housing program. He couldn't rely on one of the bigger housing funds doing anything soon. Getting a commitment out of Cathedral REIT was going to take forever and chasing them more would probably drain the life out of him. Kevin considered what other options he could explore. He needed the opposite of Cathedral REIT because they simply were not an entrepreneurial group. They seemed to be repelled by anything new or different.

While waiting for any big REIT to get on board with the program, Kevin decided to begin building a key group of several influential people who could get involved to drive public awareness, high-level policy, and eventually lead a shift in attention from the big real estate funds. He felt the bigger funds needed to get involved if he was going to attract greater funding resources. This would be a group of business and political leaders as well as some brilliant financial minds. He could even start to approach a governmental housing loan insurance association to look at a specialized policy to support this approach to housing. Reaching out to the new people Kevin had met at the gala would be a good start.

This could take time to build up, he thought. Maybe this would be the 20-year investment he had pondered aloud on the summit of their last mountain ascent. Kevin was prepared for another challenge now, and it could possibly become his full-time vocation.

It was time to start building again.

*****

Sitting on the back patio of their house in the afternoon, Jenny and Kevin got to chatting about plans again. Danny was at a friend's house and Mella was in her room on her computer. It was a warm day and the sun was out. They had just eaten lunch and were comfortable. The conversation wasn't flowing but they were keeping it alive with a little effort. Asking each other about what had happened recently with the people they each worked with brought out a few interesting stories.

At one point during a pause in the conversation the sun started glinting off the edge of a wandering cloud and the rays of light touching the patio reminded Kevin of the day on the pebble sand beach. Jenny had talked about that day several times over the years. Kevin could remember the mood on that day and had a nostalgic flashback. Kevin recalled that afternoon clearly at the time when Jenny first told him it was one of her favourite days. The strength of meaning Jenny had described for that day caused Kevin to lock it away in his memory vault too. The contrast between that afternoon on the beach and the conversation they were presently having added bitterness to an otherwise spotless memory. Now when he thought of that afternoon by the water it brought some grief. The breadth of the bond between them had narrowed and had seemed to become more brittle as time went by. The harder he tried to mend it, the more forced their marriage felt.

Just then a shriek of delight was audible from inside the house. Jenny looked up at Kevin with a smirk. Sometimes Mella's persona was draining, other times it was a joyful source of entertainment for them. They both knew she was probably connected online with one of her older friends and was giggling over something beyond her years.

Eventually the topic of kids came up. Kevin had wavered on the conversation about having another baby but still wasn't able to be persuaded to start trying again. That had chilled things between them considerably. Jenny had told him she was happier knowing they weren't going to have to move out of their home on short notice but she still worried he would become seriously injured on another mountain climb or worse. No matter what they tried to talk about the conversation always seemed laced with overtones of contempt.

Now, out of the blue, Jenny turned and asked Kevin a pointed question: "Do you still want to be married?"

"Of course," Kevin coughed after saying it, like he had choked on something.

Kevin's reaction to that question reminded him of Jenny's expression when he asked it of her before. The thought in Kevin's head was, "How dare you?" But he didn't say it out loud. In his mind, everything he had been doing was intended to rebuild the very thing she was now questioning. While he felt perilously close to accepting her ultimatum by just saying "no," as a release to his continued uncertainty, there were still a few threads strong enough to keep him holding on.

They were on their way to owning the home they lived in. Jenny was becoming a respected member of the leadership team at the hospital. Kevin had re-established a stable income which was benefiting the family. But more than anything, Kevin was trying to figure out how to once and for all erase the pain they'd experienced together.

He had a growing passion for pursuing his homeownership ideas on a bigger scale and opportunities were appearing for him all the time. He could see a path for work stretching off into the distance. But with Jenny, the path had disappeared and he was back walking in the middle of a dense forest again, unsure where to turn next or if he should just turn around and go back the other way.

PART TWO
Nine Years Later

Chapter 8
SHOCKED

Each flash of lightning was accompanied almost simultaneously by a deafening crack of thunder.

"That means the storm is really close," Danny said. "When there's no time between the lightning and the thunder. It must be right on top of us. I've never seen a storm this bad."

Kevin was thinking that he'd never seen a storm this fierce either, but he didn't want to tell his son that in case it worried him. Danny was a senior in high school. The two of them stood a few feet back from the front window, watching as the streetscape was illuminated over and over again by lightning.

It was early in the evening after sunset but some residual light gave the thick billowing storm clouds an eerie purple glow. There were ominous colours in the sky, spread out behind the violently bright white flashes of light. The lightning was striking so close that each flash left a deep red after-image when they closed their eyes.

"Are we worried about any trees falling on the house?" Danny asked.

"All the trees within striking distance of our roof are too small to do any real damage. Maybe rip off the gutters or a few shingles but the branches aren't heavy enough to structurally impact our home." Kevin tried to assuage Danny's nervousness.

Kevin and Jennifer were at home with Danny who was on spring break that week. Mella was away at university. Jenny was sharing videos with Mella of the lightning striking outside of their front window. Mella's reading week was three weeks prior so she was already through her midterm exams and looking ahead to her finals in April.

The power in the neighbourhood had been out for two hours already.

Everything was dark except for the occasional beam from the flashlight Danny held, turning it on every once in a while as if to reassure himself. He looked at the flashlight and then turned to Kevin and Jenny. "We've got spare batteries, right?" he asked.

"I'm sure there's some in the drawer," Kevin said.

"I'm just going to see how many we have," Danny said, turning on the flashlight and heading for the kitchen.

When he was out of earshot, Jenny said, "Speaking of batteries, is your phone charged? I'm at 40% and don't want to be out of touch with Mella."

"We can charge phones from the USB port in the car," Kevin reminded her.

Danny emerged from the darkness, preceded by the flashlight beam.

"These are triple A," he said, pointing the flashlight at two packages of batteries in his hand. "The flashlight takes double A."

"I'll see if I can pick some up when the storm has passed over," Kevin said.

When the rain stopped and Kevin went outside to look at the view of the city, he could see that a vast section of the landscape, including a large portion of the central business district downtown, was pitch black. Not a single visible light in the affected areas. It was frightening to see that much of the city blanketed in darkness. An important substation must have been hit, Kevin thought. This was the kind of thing that made people act compulsively, hoarding groceries and other necessities.

He would have to go and check to see if anywhere was open to buy batteries. Driving around the corner to leave the neighbourhood, Kevin noticed that the porch light was on at one of the houses on the next street over. "How do they have power?" he thought.

Driving around for a while, Kevin found everything within 20 minutes of their home in all directions closed with no backup power. Coming back into the neighbourhood, the house with the light on stood out like a beacon in the storm. Was it possible the family there had a backup generator?

Kevin turned down the street and pulled up in front of the one house that still had power on. It was like a safe haven in the storm that night. With a full view of the house, he could see that other lights were on inside too. Before getting out of the car he sent a text message to Jenny to say he was almost back at home but was going to meet a neighbour down the street who somehow had power on.

"Time to meet the neighbours," he thought as he got out to find out how this home had the lights on when nowhere else did. The house was very solid looking with a finely crafted rock facade around the front door providing a covered porch area underneath an arched opening. It was warm and inviting with a solid wood front door with finely carved dentil moulding under a small rectangular window near the top.

An older gentleman answered the door. He was clean-shaven and had light grey hair combed like a throwback to an old style. The way his hair was done reminded Kevin of someone out of the Kennedy era but it still looked distinguished on him. His tortoise-shell framed glasses were similar to a rare style that Kevin had heard were recently being custom made in Paris.

"Hello," the neighbour said, his eyes were soft but had an inquisitive look.

"Hi, I'm Kevin Robertson, I live just around the corner from you."

"Oh, it is a pleasure to meet you, my name is Max Weidman. How are you getting along with this power outage?" Max said.

"Well, that's just it. Our home is still blacked out but I noticed the lights on here and I was very curious to find out your solution?" Kevin asked. Kevin noticed how crisply Max was speaking and became more self-conscious of his own enunciation.

"Ah yes. We have a backup generator. It has good capacity too. We always like to be prepared for anything in our family."

"No kidding. That's got to be a good-size generator to power the whole house." Kevin was impressed. He had researched backup generators for the buildings where his software company had been located years before and knew they were not cheap. Buying and installing them with fail-over switches to turn on when the main power to the home was shut off was also an expensive undertaking.

"Would you like to come in and meet some of your other neighbours while we all wait for the power to turn back on?" Max offered. Kevin looked past where Max was standing in the doorway to see five other people in the living room enjoying some baked treats and what looked like red wine.

"My wife and son are at home and I just went out to check if any stores were open. I wouldn't want to leave them in the dark but thanks for the offer," Kevin politely declined.

"Of course they can join you. We would be more than happy to have all three of you over," Max said with a smile on his face.

"Ok, then. I'll go and get them and come back in a few minutes. Thank you." Kevin walked back to his car to bring back Jennifer and Daniel.

*****

When Max opened the door to his home again for Kevin, Jenny and Danny, three additional neighbours had joined the group. It looked like more people were curious about the lights being on and wanted to meet the Weidmans. After coming into the living room and making some introductions Kevin said, "You've set a good example by being so well prepared, I'm thinking it'd be good to get a generator myself. This is what emergency preparedness is supposed to look like."

Alice, Max's wife, laughed. "Well, I guess that depends on what you call an emergency," she said. "The generator manual recommends prioritizing essential items that should always be powered up. It suggests things like medical equipment, security systems and food storage appliances like freezers. That's when Max's eyes lit up and the real motive for the generator became apparent." She pointed towards the stairs to the basement, where a glowing light indicated something was powered up.

"Freezer?" Kevin asked.

"Wine cellar," Alice said. "The only real emergency around here is if the wine cellar's air conditioner is compromised."

"It's the first thing he hooked up to the generator. Our relatives like to joke that the only things that will survive an apocalypse are cockroaches and Max's wine collection," Alice said. "If a meteor hits the earth, they'd expect to find Max sitting on the patio, surrounded by a desolate landscape overrun by roaches, calmly sipping a Chablis," Alice teased.

"I'm not nearly as bad as Alice says I am," Max said. "She knows full well that I didn't get the upgrade that protects against ice ages and super volcanoes."

"Just the one for regular volcanoes," Alice said.

"Well that's just common sense, my dear," Max said, smiling and squeezing her hand.

While everyone was chatting, Kevin took a moment to talk to Max directly and asked about his background and what line of work he is or was in.

"Line of work? Well, I guess you could say I spent my career watching money. I retired three years ago from my last post as a director with the central bank," Max said.

"Well, I have never met anyone that has seen the inner workings of a central bank." He now saw Max as a very distinguished figure. "I have been curious about the central bank and what's myth and what's real so to speak. I started working on an equity sharing program for home buyers years ago and eventually switched careers from the software industry into financial services, so the effects of central banking have become more relevant to me."

"What type of financial services do you provide?" Max asked.

"I developed a way to share the equity in a home between the landlord and the tenant that was better for both," Kevin said. "Nothing against bankers, but I was struggling to get back into homeownership after I had to sell my software company for less than expected. While looking for a way to build up a downpayment to meet the mortgage rules at the time, I came up with a better way."

"I think I have heard of something like that," Max said.

"We called it Shared Equity Housing," Kevin confirmed.

"Of course, now I remember, one of my friends who sits on the board of a real estate fund mentioned it two years ago when they were looking at different ways of investing in residential real estate," Max recalled.

"That's great to hear, we can never tell how much attention our program gets from any of the real estate funds we meet."

"I am intrigued. I make it a point to try to keep up to date on new developments in the finance world," Max said. "Tell me how you got started."

Kevin started with the story of how all of the parts came together when he re-discovered the Nash Equilibrium while watching the movie about John Nash's life. Then went on to recount the steps in getting it off the ground, including working with Paul Wright for the first 10 homes.

"In fact, my own family was the test subject. We moved into the very first shared equity home," Kevin said.

He went on to describe how his family completed their contract and was able to get a mortgage to take title to the home. The mortgage rules changed again before the end of the contract period but Kevin's income had improved along the way so they finally qualified again when their share of the equity had grown enough to satisfy their down payment requirement.

Out of the other nine families who made up the original 10, six had also completed their purchases and the other three had new jobs or changes in family circumstances that forced them to move before they were ready to get a mortgage. Their homes sold and they got their share of the equity out which gave them anywhere between three times and seven times the amount of equity they began with. All of the families were happy with the program and Paul was thoroughly satisfied with his return on investment — so much so that they reinvested capital and profits in more homes, funding another 15.

While they were overseeing the first 10 homes, they learned a great deal about the unique conditions under which the program works better, and where they had to modify the legal documents to take into account specific scenarios that can occur over time. They also started to work with buyers to make sure they understood what they needed to become mortgage qualified years in advance. They made sure buyers were prepared when it was time to complete the purchase.

Two years after they started, one of the mid-sized publicly traded real estate funds decided to use their program and was the first quasi-institutional organization to begin investing in Shared Equity Housing. The fund ramped up quickly too.

Within a year they had funded over 100 homes and continued to further refine their targeting of homes in the kind of neighbourhoods where they would get the best return. This was great for the families that were sharing equity because their stake in the homes grew by more too.

After two years Paul decided to ask the real estate fund if they would buy his Shared Equity Homes from him and they agreed. Paul was paid with publicly traded shares though because he wouldn't have to pay tax on his gain until he sold the shares. He liked having the shares because it gave him personal control to sell whenever he wanted.

The first real estate fund continued to ramp up and eventually created a separate division solely focused on Shared Equity Housing. As of the day of the storm, the division had over 2,700 homes where families were sharing the equity growth with the fund. The fund also started to deal with housing developers and found that because of their size, they could get better pricing for home buyers when purchasing new homes in bulk. The builders liked it too because it reduced their marketing costs and gave them more certainty of sales, thereby reducing their risk. When the fund started buying in bulk the number of families they could match with homes every year increased significantly.

Max was nodding. "I'm guessing you started to get some attention from other funds," he said.

"That's exactly what happened!" Kevin said. "Two other real estate funds saw the first fund's financial results. Other groups started realizing it was a more scalable and manageable model, and allowed investment into higher quality newer residential real estate than their portfolios of old run-down apartment buildings. Two other funds decided to start investing in Shared Equity Housing as well."

They had asked Kevin to come in and help them set up their programs, taking the best practices from the first fund and everything that had been learned so far to roll out their investment plan. When this happened Kevin thought there was enough evidence in the market to compel the governmental housing organizations to recognize this as a new category of housing.

These big real estate funds usually had mortgages on the homes for between 45% and 60% of market value at any point in time. As the funds were a lower risk for the lenders than even a high credit-rated individual buyer, Kevin believed there should be a new class of mortgage specifically for them.

He thought that if the governmental organization granted the funds an approved owner status, that would enable them to access mortgage loans that were insured, which would greatly reduce their interest rate. Then in turn, Kevin believed the competition would drive the funds to offer a greater share of the equity growth to the families living in the home, thereby helping the families to build their equity faster.

"The real surprise came a year ago when the government housing and loan association approved a new program for insured mortgages on Shared Equity Homes," Kevin said triumphantly. "The public real estate funds that were already building their programs immediately saw their share prices rise in the public markets on the announcement. And a week later another public real estate fund announced its intention to start investing in Shared Equity Housing." That was when Kevin's phone started ringing off the hook with calls from over a dozen other groups that wanted to get into the investment strategy themselves. Some of them were private and some were public.

Along the way, some of the people Paul told about his investment in Shared Equity Housing had contacted Kevin to say they also wanted to invest using the strategy. The group of individuals that came from Paul's recommendation largely wanted to stay private and hold their real estate directly. These were individuals who preferred to avoid the volatility of the stock market. They were retired and didn't want to have to check their portfolio every day, concerned that it may have dropped in value suddenly.

"That is an amazing story," Max said and sat back as Kevin finished summarizing the key events along the way. "If you don't mind, there are a few things that come to mind that I could share with you?" Max politely asked.

"By all means, you must have more insight into these things than anyone," Kevin said, recognizing Max's experience.

Max gave him a humble nod and a warm smile.

"We were always looking at the data at the central bank, the change in living costs, the change in family income, and the trends with housing affordability over time," Max began his explanation of some of the details from all of the material published by the central bank staff.

"It's one thing to look at financial data every day, but as with anything else, it's often personal stories that bring the data to life," Max said. "For me, one of those stories was a younger colleague I knew years ago who was trying to buy his first home. His family had a long tradition of supporting each generation in homeownership, so his mother agreed to help with part of the down payment. They put a high value on homeownership, starting with his grandparents back in the 1950s. The grandmother was orphaned in the second world war and grew up without the stability of a family home. When she married, it was to a man that had also lost his father in the war. They wanted to buy a home at the time but were afraid they wouldn't be able to afford it. It was so critical to them though, that they scrimped and saved and eventually had enough for a downpayment in 1957. They took out a loan and bought a nice little home to start a family in. That home cost them $11,000 and their family income at the time was $5,500 per year. The grandmother then made it a tradition that each generation would help the next to get into a home."

"Given your familiarity with the real estate market and mortgages, I'm sure you know that the economics of buying a home has changed since my colleague's grandmother bought their house in the 1950s," Max said. "The amount of annual income it takes for the average family to buy a home has increased. Back in the 1950s, the whole purchase price was only twice a family's annual income. Now just the down payment can be that much, and the basic cost of living has gone up to the point where it is harder to save after a family covers basic living costs."

"At the Central Bank, we analyzed these trends over time. It's a sign of a greater growth rate in capital compared to the increase in family income. Credit and money supply have grown faster than wages. What we can see that has partially bridged this gap is interest rates coming down. I like your equity sharing model because it enables people to use the growth in asset values to help them save a downpayment to eventually buy a home," Max said. "That is why people say 'the rich get richer' which is true although it isn't something that we like to admit. Capital is like gravity, the more of it there is in one place, the easier it is to capture more money flowing around it."

"Based on what I have seen over the years, I have settled on some maxims that have served me well. Those maxims seem to also support what your program does to get people into homes," Max continued.

"People talk about mortgages as forced savings plans, but I prefer to think of it as automatic contributions to your net worth," he said. "You bypass all the foibles of human nature that way. And you're also appealing to another part of human nature: the part that needs the motivation of consequences. With a mortgage, you give yourself a clear goal, and a tangible reminder of that goal because you're living in your home. Savings, and most other types of investments, don't have that built-in mandatory responsibility, or those clear objectives that help people meet that obligation. There are lots of investment programs that claim to be better than building equity in the family home, but historical results don't show them being the best first place to build wealth, likely because they take more discipline than human nature provides."

As Max finished describing his principles, the lights on the homes across the street blinked on. The background noise of the generator working somewhere in the basement of the home went silent with a slight flicker of the lights in Max's home as the source switched over.

The power was finally back on.

When Jenny and Danny were ready to go Kevin turned to Max to shake his hand and thank him for sharing his thoughts. Max was more than happy to turn his mind to a new idea. Max shook Kevin's hand firmly and with purpose, then said "It was great to meet you, Kevin Robertson. I hope we can talk again soon. After I have given what you described some further thought it would be great to find a time to sit down over coffee."

"Absolutely. Anytime. Do you want to meet sometime the weekend after next? I could come by mid-morning on that Saturday and we could walk from here through the park to the coffee shop on the corner at the end of the block," Kevin answered without hesitation.

"That sounds splendid," Max said and saw the family out the door, then waved as they got into their car.

"It seemed like you were having a good conversation with Max," Jenny said as they walked to the car.

"His time at the Central Bank must have given him a bird's eye view of the financial markets. With his experience and knowledge, I'm curious what he will share after the ideas sink in." Kevin was looking forward to meeting Max again. New questions were already forming in his mind that he wanted Max's opinion on.

"I wonder what he will tell me when we meet again?" Kevin thought to himself as he pulled the car into their driveway. Danny got out and walked into the house ahead of them. Kevin then smiled at Jenny, for no particular reason. They had never really found the same bright spark they had when they first were married but they'd become more relaxed and comfortable in each other's company.

"Hey guess what?" Jenny switched to another topic.

"Yeah?" Kevin looked up.

"I am thinking of taking Danny for a trip this summer for four or five days down south just after graduation before he starts work." Jenny was grinning.

"He'd probably like that. Remember when we tried to get Mella to come with us on holiday when she was 15?" Kevin chuckled.

"Don't remind me." Jenny shook her head

"At least we don't have to worry about her being jealous," Kevin replied.

Kevin felt that Jenny hadn't connected with Danny much lately, their son had been busy with school and Jenny was now a senior executive at the hospital with a greater workload. Jenny and Mella had experienced some friction over the last couple of years as Mella started to become more comfortable making decisions for herself. Kevin was usually more willing to let Mella experience the pain of her own mistakes. He thought Jenny, however, was more protective and didn't think that Mella was mature enough not to make a terrible decision that could affect the rest of her life.

They were both uneasy over the prospect of no longer having either of their kids at home. It was an unspoken concern that they would no longer have the company of anyone but each other.

*****

On Saturday morning when Kevin was set to have his meeting with Max, he was anxious with anticipation. Kevin had been looking forward to talking with Max again and finding out what he thought would happen in the future for the financial markets.

Kevin walked over to Max's house and greeted him at the door. Max looked down at his watch and looked up and smiled at Kevin. "Good morning, I see you are right on time with one minute to spare. Excellent."

"But of course," Kevin smiled back. "Shall we?" Kevin made a swinging motion with both of his hands in the direction towards the park. Max put on a charcoal wool flat cap and closed the door behind them and they set out down the street.

Second conversation with Max…

"So Max, what got you started into the world of finance? What did you study after high school to enter the career you had?" Kevin asked.

"My father was an accountant, which gave me an early exposure to the way money works in businesses. When I got older I became more curious about the way money moved in the markets and between countries." Max said. "The more invisible aspects of the way that money flowed between the banks and the stock market and the government were a mystery to me and I wanted to see for myself. As to my education, I got an economics degree with several courses in finance and literature. I wanted to be able to understand business and communicate my ideas properly. After five years working in the treasury department at a bank I then went back to study again and completed all the requirements for my Ph.D., also in economics."

"Were you always interested in economics, even when you were growing up?" Kevin asked.

"Well, there was a while there in kindergarten when I was on the fence…" Max chuckled.

"I guess a career in central banking makes sense after hearing that story," Kevin said. "When did you get interested in wine? I'm assuming that was post-kindergarten?"

"Alice teases me about the cellar, but she enjoys it, too," Max said. "That interest developed more slowly than my interest in economics. The thing about wine is, the more you learn about it, the more interesting it becomes. That old saying, 'wine is life' is true in many ways. Every wine tells its own life story."

"A bottle of wine is constantly evolving, and always reflects its unique circumstances and environment: the grapes will always be different depending on soil and weather conditions. Fermentation itself is a biological process — a function of microorganisms going about their lives. Casks made of different materials affect wine differently. Even once it's in the bottle it keeps evolving. Any given bottle will be slightly different depending on what day you take the cork out. I guess I like the fact that wine reflects its past, its environment — it's own life."

"It's amazing to me that wine has fairly simple ingredients, but its eventual character is dependent on how it responds to several processes and situations."

"One of the things about buying wine is it makes you think ahead. If I buy a bottle that won't be at its peak for two or three years, it lets me think about what I might want to be doing then. What I might want to be celebrating, or what I might want to have accomplished by then. And that makes me think about what I need to do to accomplish those things and put things in motion for the future. When I open a bottle of wine that was made from grapes harvested three or five or 10 years ago, it's a reminder that a lot of things take time and preparation."

"Wine is not a bad metaphor for investing. If your goal is to produce good wine, you will have to plan far ahead. You will be unable to predict the weather or the harvest, but you're going to have to work with whatever the outcome is. There won't be much immediate gratification. You're going to have to put in some time and effort to ferment and store and filter and bottle it before you can enjoy the 'returns.' A nice glass of wine doesn't just spontaneously exist. It's been years in the making, just like a solid financial situation," Max said as they reached the coffee shop. He turned to look at Kevin and smiled again. "Which reminds me of your Shared Equity Housing. I imagine you're more interested in discussing homeownership than wine?"

"Let me buy you a coffee," Kevin said, opening the door for Max.

After grabbing their cups and sitting down, Kevin asked, "What is your view of homeownership? Is it just a status symbol or is there something more to it financially?"

"Since we have the time this morning let me tell you about a trip I took for a central banking conference held in Singapore 10 years ago," Max said.

"Did you say Singapore?" Kevin checked to make sure he heard correctly.

"Yes, and my story starts with the cab driver who took me to my hotel from the airport when I landed. It was my first time there but I had read a lot about it. It had already become one of the top shipping ports in the world, and was third in the world as a currency trading hub. At that time it only had a population of just over five million, but it had come from being a third world country back in the early 1960s. I had assumed that it must be an expensive place to live, and that housing must come at a premium because it's an island, so there's an absolute limit on urban expansion," Max said. "But the cab driver told me he owned his home, and he found the payments comfortable."

"Driving a taxi must pay well in Singapore," Kevin commented.

"That's what I thought. But that's not it. And he didn't inherit a big down payment either," Max said. "The taxi driver told me almost everybody in Singapore is a homeowner. I asked how people managed that, and he explained that there were programs that encouraged people to buy, and that helped make the financing comfortable. I thought that was interesting. When I bought a magazine, I asked the woman who worked at the newsstand about homes in Singapore. She was a homeowner, too."

"So I did a little research, and it turns out Singapore has a homeownership rate of over 90%. Back at the end of the 1960s, the government saw the potential benefits of homeownership and tried to offer different options to incentivize home buyers. Their initial ideas were slow to gain acceptance from 1968 through to 1971, but then they made some changes to the program. At that point it seemed to capture the citizens' interest because the number of homes they were selling took off like a rocket. They went from several hundred homes built and sold each year to building and selling 150,000 homes every five years through the 1980s."

"By 2010 they had housed over three million Singaporean residents. Looking back on the programs they started with, it was possible because they are a small island nation where the same government that controls planning and zoning, has a vertically integrated housing development and financing corporation. In the case of Singapore, they could oversee all those

activities efficiently because it was all happening locally
in one city. They think differently from other
governments around the world, though. They have a
more business-minded approach to solving problems.
They came up with their own unique ways to make it
possible for more Singaporeans to own their homes.
And it worked," Max said.

"In Singapore a lot of the real estate
development is government-driven, and there are
government programs that help people become
homeowners, all managed by what they call their
Housing Development Board or HDB," Max added.
"That level of public sector involvement might not
directly transfer to our market, but the point I came
away with was this: their approach to buying a home
and financing homeownership is different than ours,
and it makes homeownership accessible to everybody. I
started wondering if there were ways to modify our
standard home-buying process that might make it more
accessible."

"Kevin, on the night of the blackout when you
told me about the Shared Equity Housing program you
started, it made me think of what Singapore
accomplished with homeownership. They did it as a
governmental program, but their approach would be
extremely difficult for other governments around the
world to emulate. Your approach, however, is already
working here. It can continue to be managed by the
private sector, and doesn't require government subsidy.
You have effectively found a solution that can work for
larger countries to reach the level of homeownership
that Singapore has achieved."

"Wow, thank you, I guess." Kevin said. The
parallels to Singapore's success instilled greater

confidence in Kevin to keep pursuing even more widespread access to equity funding for home buyers.

"Yes, you are really onto something with this Shared Equity approach," Max said. "It's a small shift in the purchase process, but makes a seismic difference in affordability over time."

Kevin reinforced Max's statement, saying, "It makes such a difference to be building equity instead of chasing a bigger and bigger down payment. A home buyer gets to live in their home while saving for it, and they know they are closer to buying it with each month that passes. Seeing the behaviour and response from the families that were in the first group of 10, really made me understand the potential of the arrangement."

"It wasn't immediately obvious what the main problem holding people back was until we started running our advertising and had hundreds of responses to some little free ads next to the list of all the homes for rent in the city. That was when I realized that there were lots of people looking to get into homeownership, but who were having trouble putting together a down payment in a reasonable time frame," Kevin continued.

"Many families have the same motivation as ours did to make a deposit and make a payment toward their equity every month. The opportunity to move into your own home while you're still saving for it is something that most potential home buyers find very appealing: they can live in their home right now instead of paying rent on something else, and trying to build a down payment in a savings account that pays next to no interest."

"That's the beautiful thing: the problem that keeps so many people out of the housing market — inflation and rising home prices while they're trying to save a down payment — works in their favour under this arrangement," Kevin said.

"And by the way, a savings account doesn't pay next to nothing, it pays less than nothing once inflation is factored in," Max said. "In real terms, we are losing money in a savings account over the long term. If programs like your Shared Equity approach aren't available, my prediction is that it will continue to become harder and harder for people to buy homes. The price of real estate will go up in urban centres with inflation and population growth. If real family income continues to lose ground relative to the value of assets, the only thing that can be done is to slowly bring down interest rates or force people to live in smaller and smaller homes. The actual rate of borrowing will never become zero percent for an extended period of time, but the closer it gets to zero the more financing can be provided while still having monthly mortgage payments people can afford. In effect, it is a way to keep capitalism going forever. But... the amount of money needed for a downpayment will grow vastly," Max said. He had a way of putting things that made everything he said sound like it deserved to be etched in stone on the walls of a monument at a great university or museum.

"I don't know what to say to that. I never even thought about that possibility before," Kevin said, speechless.

"You are already moving in the right direction. The world's population will continue to grow past 10 billion and maybe even beyond 11 billion so we are going to have to keep building more housing and figure out a way to finance it." Max left his words hanging in the air. It had the effect of stirring up Kevin's drive to charge forward and push. More real estate funds, more developers, and more government officials had to take action.

"Thanks for buying coffee," Max said.

"You're very welcome. Like our first meeting you have given me a lot more to think about," Kevin said.

Max seemed to pause a moment at the door as they were leaving the coffee shop. "Everything ok?" Kevin asked.

Max nodded. "Everything's fine, just a little sped up," he said, slowly moving forward again. "Don't be alarmed. My heart gets a bit ahead of itself sometimes — speeds up — but it'll right itself. It's a minor complication."

"Complication?" Kevin said, sounding alarmed despite Max's reassurance.

"A minor one," Max repeated. "It happens once in a while, but there's no need to worry. Just a little heart quirk I was born with: Ebstein Anomaly. And I do mean little. Mine is a pretty minor case, since the occasional fast heart beat is the only effect it's ever had on me. Well, unless you count having to rule out a career in the NBA from a young age," he joked, putting Kevin at ease again.

"It's a good thing you had economics to fall back on," Kevin said, sensing Max would prefer not to discuss his health in detail. But he kept an eye on Max, and their pace, as they walked.

As they passed through the park on their way home, Kevin could see several young kids climbing around and running on the large multi-coloured play structure. Some older kids were playing soccer in the open field area. A few women were standing near the path talking, watching the kids running back and forth with the soccer ball. As Kevin and Max came closer to the group Kevin thought he recognized one of them.

"Sarah? Is that you?" Kevin asked. The group turned as he walked up, and as they did Kevin became certain it was her.

"Kevin Robertson, it has been a long time," Sarah responded.

"It definitely has, how long has it been now — 10 years?" Kevin said.

"Everything is good, no complaints. I heard from someone that you got into working on a new housing funding program that is doing well?" Sarah asked.

"Yes — in fact, that is what Max and I have been talking about all morning. It would be great to catch up more sometime. Do you ever see Simon around?" Kevin asked.

"Every few months. He is busy working with a new company building a technology he can't talk about with anyone. Sounds like security-related work again," Sarah replied.

"I don't know how to get in contact with Simon, would you be able to send me his new information?" Kevin asked.

"Sure, I will re-connect you with him," Sarah replied. "It's great to hear you are well."

"You too Sarah, let's stay in touch," Kevin waved and thought it was amazing to run into her again but couldn't let go of the new focus he was stuck on after everything Max had told him.

Coming out of the park, Kevin's head was spinning with ideas. What if Shared Equity funding became so popular that anyone across the country could have access to it if they needed it? What if the more their equity grew the more they would share in the equity because they became less risky for the investor and had a greater incentive to keep going? What would be the impact on a country if, like Singapore, everyone could become homeowners? Could we move towards a time when all families had enough equity to help the next generation buy a home? What if everyone ultimately paid off their homes to live free of housing payments by retirement? Was that possible in 50 or 60 years, given how long it would take for one generation to pay off their mortgages?

"Wow, what a good morning this has been," was all Kevin could say as they got close to Max's home.

"Would you look at that, Claire is here," Max said, looking at a car parked in front of his house. "If you have another minute I will introduce you to my daughter."

"Sure, happy to. I didn't know you had a daughter," Kevin answered.

When they came in the front door, a woman was in the dining room talking with Alice, but walked over to the front foyer to greet them.

"Claire, please meet our neighbour Kevin," Max said.

"Pleased to meet you," Kevin said, immediately seeing the family resemblance. She was intelligently dressed for a Saturday morning and had a very expensive looking bracelet on.

"It is a pleasure to meet you too," Claire said, echoing her father's respectfully polite manner.

"Kevin and I have just been discussing housing finance over coffee," Max added.

"Then I am sure you had my father's full attention. He can't help himself whenever anyone has something to say about finance," Claire said.

"Claire is a fund manager at a large independent money manager based here in the city. Very successful too. She probably knows many of the real estate funds you have worked with on their investment into the Shared Equity Housing strategy." Max was clearly proud of his daughter. The more time Kevin spent with Max the more he liked him.

"Yes, of course. In fact, I had heard them mention their Shared Equity investment portfolio results on their quarterly conference calls. They are doing very well with their holdings," Claire confirmed.

"That is excellent to hear. If the market is gaining confidence in the value that Shared Equity Housing creates for the real estate funds, then they will be able to expand their capacity to fund more homes, which means more people getting into homeownership," Kevin said.

"I am sure my father told you about his desire to see everyone in his family own their home. He helped me get started with ownership the first year out of university. It was a huge springboard getting into the market at that age. My first mortgage was paid off before I was 39 and I was able to keep a low mortgage balance when I moved into a larger home." Claire shared more details. "Dad, being the velvet-glove, iron-handed father that he is, provided the early equity on the basis that it was returned when the home was eventually sold. By the time I went to sell that first home though, my father's initial equity was a small amount of the total sale proceeds so it was very easy to move up to a bigger home."

"The one fundamental difference between owning a home and renting is that if we don't ever buy a home and pay off the mortgage, we will always have to make a monthly payment for housing," Max said.

"No guaranteed return is greater than a mortgage payment on that same amount of investment. Banks simply don't work that way. The only way to have a true financial guarantee in retirement is to own a home and have paid off the mortgage. Then we don't need as much in our investment portfolios to ensure we will always have a home to live in while we are alive."

"Speaking of which, there are a few people I know who haven't been able to get into the housing market yet. I will pass along the name of your company to them," Claire said.

"By all means, we always appreciate referrals," Kevin replied.

"Thank you again, Max. It was great meeting with you this morning. And Claire, it is wonderful meeting you." Kevin was not sure if he would cross paths again with her but was happy to have more contacts to expand his network in the financial markets. He would have to build an even bigger personal circle of relationships for what he was thinking of doing next. He also hoped that he would be able to meet with Max again soon. He was nearly walking on air after the infusion of ideas from their chat over coffee.

Chapter 9
KISS

By the time he got home, Kevin was thinking this was no longer a matter of a single funding step to get buyers started. It could be a whole spectrum of financing options. There were more ways to improve people's ability to grow their equity with greater financial stability at every stage in the homeownership life cycle. Just as Singapore had set up its Housing Development Board (HDB) to get people into a home the moment they became engaged to be married, and gave them financial solutions for life stages from their first child all the way through retirement, the same could be done building off the Shared Equity program. All of it possible by harnessing the equity in their homes.

Kevin could see other ways of expanding in all directions from what the real estate funds were already doing. On top of that, by having all of these big real estate funds invested in the housing market, there would be ways of offering homeowners the ability to reduce their risk of untimely home value fluctuations — such as when they need to sell to move to another home, for example. The greater the variety of financial interests in the housing market, the more that risks could be spread out.

"Jenny? Where are you?" Kevin shouted, louder than he needed to but he was too excited to care. "I just had a mind blowing talk with Max."

"I am over here," Jenny called out from the den, where she was catching up on some work. She was now executive director of the hospital, which had also undergone several more expansion projects over the last five years and was operating better than ever.

"Max is a brilliant guy. Amazingly, we have been neighbours with him for years but it took the most terrifying storm in the city's history to put us in touch." Kevin shared highlights of the discussion with Max and tried to relate the problems that still needed to be solved as well as the opportunity as he saw it.

Kevin thought it was time to go and see the investment bankers. He didn't want to meet with just anyone, he needed to find a 'wizard.' Someone like Max who had spent a career trying to solve difficult problems with complicated subjects, but this person would need to be an expert at designing financial investment products for major pension funds and global investors. He didn't want to just deal with the existing real estate funds that owned all different types of commercial real estate. They only held a small portion of their portfolios in shared equity housing. He knew the total value of residential housing real estate was equal to or greater than all publicly traded companies combined in the majority of the developed world. In their country it was a market approximately equal in size to their entire economy. Residential real estate was five times bigger than all types of commercial real estate put together, so if residential housing was addressed properly it could lead to real estate funds that had five times the assets of the commercial real estate groups that existed.

The funds had already started to benefit from mortgage insurance but there was so much more to be done to expand upon the transitional mortgage products new real estate funds could also offer to accelerate their homebuyers' progress.

Kevin wondered if Max or Claire might know of someone within their networks that could be the person he was looking for. Kevin decided he should follow up with Max sooner rather than later, once he had his thoughts organized.

*****

Kevin thought he would surprise Max with a gift. After speaking with some friends who were knowledgeable about wine, he bought a bottle of Chateau Margaux vintage 2005 that typically only people like Max would appreciate. Max opened the door but didn't quite look like his usual precisely groomed self. His hair didn't have the normal sheen to it and the skin around his eyes seemed darker than before. He was clean-shaven but didn't have the twinkle Kevin remembered seeing when they went for coffee.

"Good afternoon," Kevin said with a smile. Max smiled back, showing a resolve not to let a lack of sleep temper his mood. Kevin then moved his arm around from behind his back to reveal the carefully selected bottle of wine.

"I brought a gift for you. Our talk over coffee made my mind spin with new ideas so I thought I would thank you for the inspiration." Kevin reached out to hand him the bottle.

"A 2005 Margaux, so you did remember our discussion. This is one of my favourites." Max's gaze lingered for a while admiring the bottle in his hands.

When Max finally looked up at Kevin, his spirit had lifted. "It feels like a nice day for a walk. Would you care to join me?"

"Of course. Now?" Kevin said, taken aback.

"Why yes, let me get my hat." Max returned to the front door after a moment with his brown suede jacket on and his flat cap. It was still warm outside so Kevin wouldn't have thought a jacket was needed, but he wasn't going to bring it up with him.

Third conversation with Max...

They walked to the end of the block before Max started to speak. When he did though, he sounded prepared.

"There are at least three Nobel Prize winners that have completed work over the years whose ideas support the basis for the housing funding programs you are developing, Kevin," Max said. "There is Hernando De Soto, author of *The Mystery of Capital*, whose research showed how registering the ownership of a home within a land titles system — thereby allowing it to secure financial instruments — unlocked the financial capital in the land and physical building that would be invisible otherwise. There is Robert Schiller, who created the urban home price indices and advanced so many ideas around the financial value in homes as well as pointing out the way the stock markets had been disconnected from the equity value in the housing markets. And of course, there is John Nash, who as you mentioned may have unknowingly provided the framework for a financial market solution to housing 70 years before its time when he published his papers about bargaining between two parties."

Max was getting at the 'basic principles' for what governed the financial characteristics of housing. Talking to him was like digging down through all of the noise and rhetoric found in the news to reach bedrock and truly understand why a thing worked.

"All of these things tie together when housing is layered over top of the banking system," Max continued. "If the equity in homes can be unlocked and made liquid instantly through the broader financial system and public stock markets, then it will increase the speed of money beyond what we have seen in the past."

"Speed of money?" Kevin repeated.

"There are times when lots of people and businesses are borrowing money to do things that grow the economy: things like expanding businesses, making investments, creating new products, or building a new condo tower," Max said. "Other times, people are cautious and keep money stuffed under the mattress, figuratively speaking. It is simply sitting in their bank accounts in case they need it for something else. When people are spending and borrowing and expanding and building, money moves around quickly." Max was doing his best to explain a career in central banking in everyday terms.

"The staff at the Central Bank track all of this activity to support steady, but stable consistent growth over time. Whenever it falls off or speeds up too fast, the Central Bank takes action to correct its course."

"What your new program does is start to bring the equity value of homes into the public stock markets which are also in the domain of the banks. Mortgage securities have been traded for decades but equity in housing hasn't ever made it to the liquid markets. When it does, it will naturally create more flow of money because it will unlock, or 'monetize' as bankers say, the equity that normally can only be accessed when a family sells their home to move. Then when they settle into their new home it is locked right back up again."

"Just so that I am understanding you, are you saying that connecting housing equity into the stock market through the Shared Equity Program will increase the movement of money?" Kevin needed to make sure he understood Max.

"Correct!" Max said. "Technically, innovation and businesses growing each year will do the same but the size of the housing market is so large that its contribution will be significant."

"What will that mean for the central bank in the future?" Kevin was starting to catch up to what Max was saying.

"Depending on how the economy is functioning, the central bank will raise or lower interest rates. To get the economy moving faster, the central bank can lower interest rates. When the cost of borrowing money is low, people are more likely to borrow money to buy a car, or to borrow more money to buy a more expensive car. People are more likely to get a loan to buy assets because it would be easier to get a return that is greater than the cost of the loan. They're more likely to get a loan to start a business, or, if they already have a business, to expand their product line and hire more people. All of which stimulates the economy."

"As interest rates rise, so does the cost of borrowing money to do all of those things, which means fewer people borrow money, and people tend to borrow lower amounts. By raising interest rates, the central bank takes its foot off the gas and may even put on the brakes. Or by lowering rates and having the economy speed up it is also likely to lead to more

inflation. So when the rate comes down, owning a
home will mean inflation starts to increase its value
(along with rent) but not increase the monthly
mortgage payment."

"It may also decide to increase the amount of
money moving around between people and the banks.
A central bank can do that. They will continue to adjust
to whatever stress is found in the markets," Max went
on with the line of thinking.

"If the central bank is increasing the money
supply, effectively increasing the amount of credit that's
available, it's trying to stimulate the economy. Making
new money isn't the only tool they use to do that. But
there are times when injecting new money into the
economy — we call it liquidity — can help."

"You make new money and give it to the
banks?" Kevin had heard it described as printing
money which didn't seem to be a useful metaphor
anymore now that physical currency was largely out of
circulation. He hoped Max would be able to put it into
terms that would be more relatable.

"No, we don't just make it, and we're not giving,
we're buying. The banks are selling us something —
bonds — and we're paying them for it," Max said. "The
bank takes the funding obtained from the central bank,
so in turn it can lend money to people and businesses,
and that money starts to circulate in the economy. That
creates more activity — more money moving faster
helps to create employment and increase incomes, but
increases inflation too. Governments accept inflation
because it increases the tax base. The markets accept
inflation because it creates the perception of a greater
return on investments."

"So injecting new money into the economy is a
pretty useful ploy," he said. "But the tactic the central

bank has at its disposal that affects real estate most directly is controlling interest rates."

"The thing about central banks — well, this is probably true of all banks — is that they are often looked upon with a bit of unease, and that's usually rooted in misunderstanding," Max said. "And I can see why people would be wary of banks. If you're going to hand your paycheck over to someone every week for safekeeping, you're going to want to be sure it is all on the up and up. So people need to know that banks are trustworthy — especially when they know that banks use their deposits in loans to other people to turn a profit."

"But when you're talking about central banks, it gets a little murkier. Whose bank are they? They're not my bank. They're not my neighbours' bank. They don't have branches or ATMs. No, they're the banks' bank, or the government's bank. Which, depending on the mood you're in, might make people even warier of a central bank."

"Because of the way central banks and our government work, inflation is necessarily part of the arrangement." Max paused there and took a deep breath. "The data shows that over the last 60 years, there was not one single year where inflation was negative. It has averaged approximately 2% each year, raising prices without fail."

"And, the research of the Nobel prize winner, Robert Schiller, showed that housing prices follow inflation over time."

"Do you remember when we spoke the first time during the storm and I said that the cost of homes has grown faster than family income? Well, this is a problem for families that lowering interest rates can help towards making monthly mortgage payments more affordable, but won't help when it comes to the down payment. If the trend over the last 60 years continues for another 30 years, and I don't see why it won't, then your Shared Equity Housing option may become essential for people looking to buy a home for the first time."

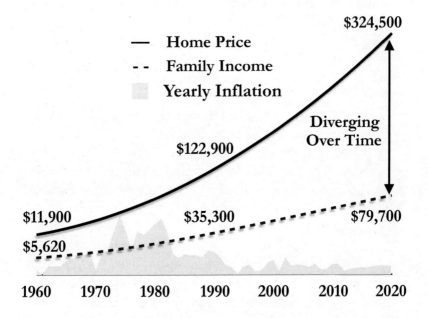

"Let me sum it up this way," Max said, turning to Kevin. "There are steps that people can take to prosper in an economy driven by capitalism with a central banking system. Missing out on those key steps leaves you in a less favourable financial position. Having an equity interest in a home is certainly one of those steps."

Kevin had to walk in silence for a little while to ponder what Max had just explained. "How is it that there has been no large-scale effort put into funding home equity before, given the economic potential in housing?" Kevin wondered aloud, still baffled.

"I have thought about that point since the first time you described your plan at our house. All that I can say is that change and advancement take time. Each layer of improvement has to be added before the next is identified. In real estate and banking, sometimes change can take a long time to spread before it becomes a new standard. It could be as simple as reaching the moment in time when the opportunity became ripe." Max was slowing down but they were getting closer to home.

Instead of lightness and excitement about what the future may hold, after this particular meeting with Max, Kevin couldn't help but feel some weight. It wasn't overwhelming in the sense that he was facing a potential crisis, but he saw that there was a responsibility to work at improving the access to equity so that more people would be able to avoid the crushing force of inflation over time. Knowing what had happened over the last 30 years with home prices and family income, Kevin thought that if those same trends continued, it would be unimaginably difficult for people to ever get into a home they could own. If they didn't they would suffer the cost of rent and monthly payments that would keep rising or they would be forced to live in far inferior housing.

*****

Sitting at the kitchen table at home after the walk with Max, Kevin's head was reeling from the implications. Kevin went immediately to his desk in the den and began writing some notes and ideas to add detail to plans he could pursue. After about an hour of thinking and writing, he was ready for a break to clear his mind. He thought suddenly of the taste of his favourite rooibos tea. Walking over to the kitchen he found Jenny enjoying a latte and reading a book. As Kevin finished getting his tea ready, Jenny happened to stand up to get a snack from the cupboard near where Kevin was standing. While waiting for his tea to steep, he leaned over to kiss her.

Jenny pulled away for a moment, which caused Kevin's heart to lurch for a half-second, leaving him unsure what to do next. He had a fleeting thought come to mind of the rockiness in their relationship before moving into this home they now owned. But then she leaned back towards him with a grin on her face. She was reading him and at that moment he realized what she was doing, she was testing him to see if he was serious about wanting to kiss her.

They embraced each other but the kiss ended rather abruptly.

The impatience of the kiss made it little unnerving, straining the precarious balance of the moment.

Their relationship felt stronger and was filled with more frequent positive days than it had for several years, but there was still an lingering tension. Their tempered affection kept them from a feeling of true satisfaction.

Chapter 10
IN A BLINK

Kevin left home in his car to go and get a couple of bottles of wine for dinner and the weekend. Driving past the end of the block now it had become a habit to look around the corner towards Max's house. Kevin found it reminded him of the heady conversations the prior week with Max, and renewed the invigorating sense of purpose he got from thinking of all the possible ways to expand the homeownership business.

This time when he looked down Max's street, there were two large, unfamiliar black vehicles parked out front. It gave Kevin a premonition that something wasn't right. He felt unsettled by it but wasn't clear what was going on.

On the way to the liquor store that Max had recommended for their wine selection, Kevin tried to think about the kind of wine that he would buy. He had picked up a few ideas from Max, and had gained a new curiosity for wine stemming from some of Max's passion wearing off on him. Not wanting to be thought of as a neophyte when it came to wine, Kevin was careful in making his selection at the store and had even read up on many wineries before going out to buy the bottles that night.

Kevin thought he would get one bottle of the Chateau Margaux to try himself, after seeing Max's reaction to the bottle he'd given him as a gift. He hoped that a new shipment of Harlan Estates may have arrived as he had his name on the list for it and wanted to surprise Jenny since she was a fan of the California Cult brands.

The black SUV's were still there when he drove past on the way home and there were a few people on Max's front porch talking with whoever was standing in the doorway behind the stone archway.

Kevin felt like there was something very strange happening, but he also knew Max was a smart guy and would sort out everything without help from his neighbours.

*****

It wasn't until the next day that Kevin discovered that this was something that Max could not sort out. Kevin was outside dealing with a leak in the watering system when one of the neighbours who had been at Max's the night of the blackout passed by walking his dog. He waved at Kevin from the sidewalk.

"Oh hello," Kevin said. "I remember you from Max's."

"I remember you too," he said. "It's so sad what happened."

"You mean the blackout?" Kevin asked, puzzled.

"No. I meant Max," he said. "I'm sorry, I thought you already knew. Max died yesterday. Heart attack."

It suddenly became clear what the black SUVs and the people on Max's porch meant.

"Alice called an ambulance, but he had stopped breathing by the time the paramedics got there."

"That's... awful," Kevin's eyebrows went taut and he had a metallic taste in his mouth slowly beginning to process the news. The neighbour kept speaking but his words were now in the background like the sound of a voice coming out of an old radio. Kevin was faintly aware of what he was saying while experiencing flashbacks in reverse order of his meetings with Max.

As Kevin's attention returned to the neighbour he heard him say, "It's tragic but he would probably say his heart lasted longer than he thought it would. He used to talk about his heart defect with me because we have the same cardiologist. He told me he didn't let it get in the way of life decisions, except to make sure he celebrated everything."

"Talk about taking the best of us first. Max was such a great guy." The neighbour finished speaking as Kevin's final flashback ended with him walking up Max's front steps during the power outage to meet him for the first time.

"I had no idea." Kevin could feel tears forming in his eyes but was able to restrain himself from breaking down in front of his neighbour. "That's just awful. Is there going to be a service?"

"I'm not sure but if you like I can ask Alice and then let you know," he said as his dog pulled at its leash.

Dazed, Kevin went inside to sit down.

*****

Max seemed to have affected many lives. So many people attended the service that every pew was full and mourners were standing three rows deep at the back and even spilling out of the doorway and still more who waited outside during the service. Those who waited outside would have a chance to come in and pay their respects once the formal service had ended. There were well over 250 people inside and from the looks of it another hundred or more people outside. Kevin had not appreciated the breadth of the impact Max had on the community between the number of boards he'd sat over the years and the philanthropic work that he had done. He seemed to affect everyone he came into contact with, leaving them with the same loyalty and reverence Kevin had experienced only knowing Max for three weeks. By the end of their third conversation, it felt like Max was someone that Kevin had known for his entire life. Yet, he'd only spent a total of seven hours with him on three different occasions.

Kevin saw Claire at the funeral and spoke with her for a moment to wish her his condolences. Claire didn't seem to be crying at the time although Alice's face was glistening with a stream of tears down her cheeks. Claire had a look of cold steel on her face as if she had tucked away all of the pain with stoic resolve, proving to Max one last time that she was strong enough to assume her father's mantle.

The eulogy was primarily given by Alice's older brother who was born the same year as Max. He spoke about Max coming to pick up Alice for their first date, and told heartwarming stories about Max. Kevin felt very lucky to have met Max and to have had the chance to be graced by his wisdom. Alice's brother mentioned Max's three primary charities that he supported with a significant portion of his income each year. One of the three happened to be the Heart and Stroke Foundation.

Kevin made a mental note of the charities along with some of the other life experiences that people felt were defining moments for Max. Everyone there was thankful for having had help, or advice, or just a kind word from the ever patient, well-mannered Max Weidman.

*****

The Monday after the funeral they got a call from their daughter Mella. Kevin and Jenny hoped that Mella would befriend a person who could be her 'lighthouse' at university to keep her from crashing against the rocks that were bound to be lurking below the waterline during her freshman experience. With just over a month left before Mella's exams, they learned that Mella had found a light, but then had smashed it that very morning, leaving her in darkness again.

Kevin and Jenny were shocked to discover that Mella had a boyfriend, which was her first, and that they had been together for a couple of months. They met in one of her first semester classes but didn't share any in the second semester. They had had a fight over something that Mella was stuck on, and he couldn't understand why she was being so stubborn. He had stormed out of the residence where Mella lived. That happened Sunday night, the day before.

Then earlier that morning during the second class of the day, Mella was seated next to one of the boyfriend's buddies. He started talking to her and tried to stir the pot by showing her messages her boyfriend had sent the buddy with a photo. The picture showed him hanging out with a big group later Sunday night and was standing with his arm around another girl's shoulders.

At least they knew that Mella was being honest with them. She was nearly in tears when she told them she screamed at the guy at the top of her lungs and the whole auditorium of students in the class stopped watching the professor and turned to look. When she saw the whole room staring at her she grabbed her bag, stood up and took a step to leave, then before running out turned to the guy and swore at him.

"Dad, can I come home for a couple of days?" Mella asked on the call.

"You don't need to come home. Just take a day off and watch some of your favourite shows or go for a walk and you'll be fine," Kevin said.

"Ya, Mella, flying home right now doesn't make sense," Jenny tossed out.

"No, you guys don't get it. If I have to go back into another lecture, I am going to scream!" Mella was already screaming into the phone.

"Okay, okay. Let me see what we can do," Kevin acquiesced.

"Thanks dad. Bye." Mella's tone had changed back to her overly cheery self in a snap and then she hung up abruptly. That wasn't the first time they had seen her do that. But they knew she could just as easily go the other way and break down entirely, sobbing or ranting and raving uncontrollably.

"Do you really think that flying her home is best?" Jenny said to Kevin after they were certain their call was over.

"I am never sure with Mella, she can be so volatile at times. Maybe if we fly her back home for a couple of days then she will be reminded of why she wanted to go to that university in the first place," Kevin said.

"Mella should just tough it out and get back to class so she doesn't miss anything important." Jenny played devil's advocate in a lot of the discussions they had. A contrarian approach seemed to be the way with many of their conversations. Kevin wondered why she did that so often. Then he thought that maybe he had been doing the same thing without noticing.

*****

Kevin went out on his own to pick up Mella from the airport and found the flight had arrived right on time. He gave her a hug and brought her bag out to the car to head home. Mella's face wore the expression of a soldier ready for battle.

When they sat down in the car and started driving, Mella pulled the pin on an even bigger grenade by saying, "I'm not going back to school."

"Ah," Kevin repeated a few times with a dumbfounded look on his face.

"Uhm,

"Well,

"What do you mean?" he said finally still not accepting her verdict.

"There is no point going back to finish my exams," Mella cooly stated.

"Tell you what," Kevin was trying to hold back. "Let's talk about it later. Relax at home for the day then I want to hear more about how your classes have been going the last few months."

"Whatever. I'm still going to have the same answer for you." Mella didn't have a hint of doubt in her voice. Kevin left the conversation hoping it wouldn't come up again and didn't mention her comment to anyone else.

After two days at home enjoying the peaceful quiet compared to the ongoing socializing at the residence on campus, Mella was recharged and independent again. Coming home allowed her to see the contrast between her new life and the one she had detested in high school. It also showed Kevin that Mella needed to have her own space; in the future he would make sure she had a home of her own of course.

Jenny, though, wanted to hear nothing of Mella missing out on the rest of the term and her exams.

After they were nearly finished eating breakfast the third day after Mella had been home Jenny took a deep breath, preparing for a jump into the deep end with Mella. "Are you ready to head back to school now?" Jenny said firmly looking Mella right in the eyes.

"What are you talking about Mom," Mella answered, not meaning it to be a question.

"The rest of the semester is paid for," Jenny said.

"So. That's fine," Mella responded, not seeing what that had to do with anything.

"People go through breakups at school but it doesn't stop them from finishing their courses," Jenny added, increasingly tense.

"None of my courses matter. I don't even know why I decided to go there in the first place." Mella was withdrawing from the conversation.

"What are you talking about? You picked all of your courses following your favourite subjects in high school." Jenny was speaking louder and becoming more flustered.

"You have no idea!! This is bull—" Mella was interrupted by Jenny who was now teetering on fury.

"I have no idea? I have no idea?!" Jenny wouldn't let Mella respond. Mella slammed the backs of her legs against her chair as she got up and left the table in a hurry towards her old room. Kevin spoke overtop of Jenny while reaching to grab Mella's wrist as she walked past but she was too quick.

"Mella! We still need to talk about this!" He then turned to look at Jenny.

"What are you doing? When has she ever responded to us when we yell at her?" Kevin found himself defending Mella although he, too, had yelled at her many times. He definitely believed she couldn't stop school but had changed his mind in the past having been convinced by Mella's stubbornness.

"Looks like I am the only one going to stand their ground with her," Jenny said, unconsciously balling her fists at her sides as she spoke, thinking that Kevin would give in and let Mella stay home. Danny had finished eating and probably sensing the conversation was escalating, he took his dishes to the counter and silently walked out of the room.

Kevin: "What is that supposed to mean?"

Jenny: "Take a guess."

Kevin: (adversarially) "I don't need to guess. Tell me."

Jenny: "You always just do what she wants," she snapped. "She knows if she's resistant enough then she'll get what she wants from her dad."

Kevin: "You think it would be better for us to yell at her and try to discipline her into going?"

Jenny: "Only if it was that easy."

Kevin: (agitated) "How do we know that she hasn't found something of greater interest?"

Jenny: "I had two break-ups during college before we met. The thought never entered my mind that I wouldn't keep going with school. My dad would have torn me to pieces if I even suggested it, not that I ever would have."

Kevin: "What the hell? None of that matters to her."

Jenny: "Why did you fly her home then?"

Kevin: "I'd rather have her here then leaving her to fall into a downward spiral in her dorm room."

Jenny paused, breathing more naturally, then said "So what do you want to do then?"

Kevin: "We can give her the morning, then I will try to talk to her and see if she will provide any more background on what she's thinking. You know how she can be."

Jenny: "Yeah, right."

When Kevin came back from work for the day he found Mella in her room. She hadn't eaten any lunch so he fixed her one of the simple meat and cheese sandwiches she used to like when she was younger. Jenny hadn't arrived back home from her day yet so he sat down on Mella's bed to talk to her. She was still facing her computer screen absorbed in something she was reading about.

Suddenly she turned around towards him and said, "Do you know how many people around the world are considered stateless? There is no record of them existing in any country. They don't have access to health care or even basic human rights."

"Where is this coming from?" Kevin was taken aback.

"The U.N. estimates that there are more than 10 million people around the world who have no legal identity. But — how could they know? By definition they are trying to count something that isn't there, with no records as proof," Mella said. Kevin furrowed his eyebrows, wondering how she was always so precocious.

"What does that mean to you?" Kevin had to ask.

"There is nothing I can see doing with my science courses that I care about. There are too many human rights issues internationally for me to ignore," Mella said matter-of-factly.

"Are you sure? When are you thinking you would do this?" Kevin was startled by her abruptness. He'd never seen her change her mind so drastically before. It made him consider that she was probably more serious about it than he could imagine.

"Right away. I am going to finish one of my current courses that will still qualify for the program going forward and then register in courses for the summer and stay on campus to catch up lost time."

"And you've checked it all out?" Kevin was beginning to realize just how serious she was.

"Yes. I have already completed all the forms to start the process." Mella was becoming irritated that he kept asking her questions like he didn't believe her.

"Wow, all right, I will go and tell your mom. I am proud of you Mellissa, this is a big cause and an important undertaking," Kevin said and gave her a hug. Kevin knew at that point she wouldn't be convinced otherwise, and was partly worried for her as statelessness was going to be a challenging issue to tackle, but he was also impressed with her and who she was becoming.

*****

By the end of that week, Kevin had started to look back on the month's whirlwind of events that had shaken up his life. Putting them in perspective he thought back to some of the other dramatic episodes that had occurred as the kids were growing up. The stress and strain that he and Jenny had gone through after he lost his business, and then when they lost the house his frustration seemed to radiate outwards to affect the kids too. He could associate the more exaggerated acts of defiance that Mella initiated around the times when there was strife at home. The struggle with the emotion of the kids and the hurdles faced going through past financial difficulties left scars that would glow hot every time he and Jenny argued.

Now he was imagining a future more clear and vivid than he'd been able to picture at any time prior in his life. He was filled with volition to initiate change in a way he never would've dared before. Everything Max shared with him was the exact set of ideas Kevin needed to see how all the remaining pieces of his grand puzzle would come together.

While wrapping up a few last tasks on his computer before finishing off for the day Kevin logged into a charity donation aggregator website.

Kevin quietly made a substantial donation to each one of Max's three charities in Max's name. Even though Max was gone, his impact on the world would continue to show signs of his presence. Kevin never mentioned the donation to anyone, because that's how Max would have done it.

Before leaving his desk for the night, he finished visualizing the solution that would account for all of the questions raised in his discussions with Max. Kevin resolved to bring together the resources for the creation of a new, pure, Shared Equity Housing fund. He believed that a new class of residential housing funds could rise to a level of preeminence above anything that had previously existed. It was the answer to matching what Singapore had achieved but in larger countries at greater scale.

Jenny was reading a book in bed when Kevin walked into the bedroom. He wasn't actively trying to avoid conversation but didn't try to interrupt her reading. Her hands and the book flopped down on top of the duvet as she looked over at him.

"Mella seems determined, doesn't she. Maybe she has finally found her calling?" Jenny said.

"I sure hope so. She's acting like an adult at least. Proactively deciding what she wants her future to hold. Handing the details herself." Kevin wouldn't admit that it felt like uncomfortable new territory to him but he was proud of her at the same time.

"It's a relief to see her get back to school. I am glad that you had the talk with her," Jenny volunteered.

"With any luck, it will work out this time." Kevin didn't need to say you're welcome and Jenny hadn't said thank you, but it was pretty close. Either way, it was a step in the right direction.

PART THREE
Twelve Years After That

Chapter 11
CONTRACTIONS

Jenny picked up her phone. She was sitting in the car with Kevin on their way out for dinner. When she answered she said, "Hi Mella," in a cheerful tone, but after going silent for a moment, her tone switched to show great concern for what she was hearing.

"Are you sure you that's what it is?" Jenny asked. "Ok, uh-huh, all right. No, keep talking," Jenny was speaking in fragments while Mella must have been frantically telling Jenny what was going on and asking questions about what she should do at the same time.

"What's going on?" Kevin tried to interrupt them to get a hint of what was happening.

Jenny put her hand over the mic and whispered, "Mella thinks she is having contractions."

"What? But she is still seven weeks away?" Kevin said, now sounding frantic himself.

"I know, but she has to go to the hospital now, either way she has to be sure." Jenny hurried to complete her sentence before turning her ear to the phone again. "Yes, okay. I agreed with you, just go and we will come to meet you there as soon as we can." Jenny put the phone away and gave Kevin the rest of the details including that Mella was having contractions about every 15 minutes. With her due date being seven weeks away and the fact that this was her first pregnancy they were all worried about what could go wrong. Mella was now on her way to "Jenny's" hospital with her husband Mark. Mark's last name was Evans which Mella had taken when they married.

Kevin looked over at Jennifer's face and raised his eyebrows slightly, not needing to say anything to know what Jenny wanted to do next. Jenny nodded slightly up and down twice with a decisive look on her face. "We're going to the hospital," he thought and prepared to change their destination. He spoke to his vehicle to confirm their change of plans and also to cancel the reservation at the restaurant. The vehicle responded immediately changing lanes and heading off down a side street. Something was happening with Mella which he knew caused Jenny to be extra vigilant. Kevin thought that maybe it was some of Mella's compulsive tendencies creating paranoia but the contractions couldn't be ignored. It was way too early for her with seven weeks still to go before her due date. Jenny's arm was resting on her lap and Kevin saw her squeeze her forearm against her abdomen twice while they were driving over to the hospital but decided not to question her about it. Kevin felt like he wanted to swallow but the muscles that would normally start peristalsis were seized by the tension he was already carrying in his throat.

*****

When they got to the hospital they were able to park in Jenny's reserved spot. They rushed inside to the wing in the hospital for expecting mothers. Jenny was quite comfortable moving through the halls there and people who she knew greeted her as she whisked by with Kevin following closely behind. Jennifer was known personally or from her photo by everyone that worked at the hospital and she would get a warm VIP treatment from anyone they saw there. She was set to retire next year from the role of Executive Director but had committed to staying on the board of directors for both the hospital and the hospital foundation which continued to gather funds for expansion projects and new programs.

Kevin still felt lost in this place whenever he came to meet or see Jenny. Today, however, he couldn't even focus on remembering the way that they had come or where Jenny was leading him. All he could think about was Mella and what she was going through.

When they arrived at the check-in counter where families of new mothers were required to sign in, both of the women behind the desk warmly greeted Jenny and Kevin. They understood immediately what Jenny was going to ask before she spoke and signalled for one of the nurses to come over right away.

"Hi, Jennifer," the nurse said without hesitation when she walked up. People who worked at the hospital never called her Jenny, but she also didn't permit people the formality of Mrs. Robertson. The nurse knew who Jennifer was but Kevin couldn't make out her name on her ID because of the angle at which she was standing. Without waiting for Jenny to ask, the nurse started to give her a rundown on what was happening and the status of Mella and the baby. "Mellissa is in her delivery room along with her husband. The doctor has already been in to see her twice and we have been paying close attention to their heart rates. We understand this is early for her, but she is well along the way now with contractions happening just over 10 minutes apart."

Just then Mark came walking over to where they were with a frightened look on his face. "Ah um. Something is happening. I think Mellissa's water has just broken," Mark said to the nurse in a panic, he had always called her by her full name, never picking up the shorter version they used as a family. Mark was still breathing anxiously and then turned to realize for the first time that the people standing next to the nurse were Jenny and Kevin. "Oh, hi Mrs. Robertson, sorry, didn't see you come in."

"Where is she, Mark?" Jenny said. Her stilted request made Mark react, he turned and waved his hand in a motion that meant for them to follow. He led them around the corner into one of the delivery rooms where Mella was lying down on the bed, breathing vigorously. The sheet and the bottom of her hospital gown was soaked from below her thighs down towards her feet. Kevin listened to the nurse ask Jenny a couple of questions and then he stooped down near Mella's shoulder to give her some words of encouragement. A few minutes later when he was seated on the couches in the waiting area, he couldn't recall anything the nurse had said or what he had told Mella to make her feel better.

A few minutes after that, Kevin heard a distant repetitive beeping sound start. A moment later a doctor hurried by heading into the delivery room. Then another doctor went by with another nurse in tow. Kevin was on the edge of his seat and wanted to go back in but they had been told it would be better to wait outside the delivery room. Jenny came out 25 minutes later looking dishevelled. With perspiration on her forehead, she tried to explain between catching her breath that the baby experienced a big "d-cell" which was a label given to seeing a baby's heart rate drop down to dangerous levels. Jenny's face was drained of colour and her expression was drawn out in concern as she finished relaying what she'd heard.

"Mella is dilated, with shorter gaps between contractions but it looks like the baby is in breech which is likely from being premature. They are going ahead with an emergency C-section to try to save the baby."

Kevin felt dizzy hearing this, worried and wishing that time would just pass by so he could be sitting next to Mella and the baby, knowing they were safe and sound. Jenny went back in to stay with her until she was under anesthesia. Then, they would both wait together, praying for a successful delivery.

*****

After taking what seemed like too long to hear back, the nurse that had met Jenny upon their arrival came back out of the delivery room looking tired. But as she got closer they could see the hints of a reserved smile on her face.

"What happened?" Jenny said.

"The operation was successful and the mother is healthy. The baby was born just shy of four pounds and is in good health except for difficulty breathing. The baby was immediately hooked up to a breathing support device that will push a mixture of air and oxygen in and out of the baby's lungs, doing the work of breathing for her. She is going to be kept in an incubation chamber for a while until we see her breathing improve," the nurse said matter-of-factly using her best bedside manner.

"So it's a girl? And she will be all right?" Kevin stammered out.

"Yes, she should be all right. All of the other initial tests show positive results and we have treated many premature babies with similar conditions to find they grow without complication. We will continue to keep a close eye on her. In a few minutes, Mellissa should be ready to see you."

"Thank you. Thank you," Jenny said. The nurse nodded with a slight bow, happy to have been able to help Jennifer's family.

*****

The issues kept the baby in the hospital for 19 days until she was breathing on her own and the mustard colour in her skin had disappeared once she was no longer suffering from jaundice. While Mella was staying at the hospital with the baby, recovering and monitoring the baby's progress, Jenny decided to stay there too. She took some time off work but being that she was around the hospital all day anyway she still checked in with her staff throughout the day.

Once Mella had taken the baby home and was becoming comfortable as a new mother, Jenny was then able to sleep at home too. That first night lying in bed next to Kevin again, Jenny started to describe her experience of watching Mella go through her frightening emergency childbirth.

"She almost lost the baby and could have suffered far worse health risks herself," Jenny said, still sounding shaken. As Jenny continued to talk about what she saw happening and what the experience meant to her, Kevin recognized that she was sharing a moment of realization with him. Jenny explained that looking back now, she saw that there could have been greater complications if they had a third baby. The pain they both went through at the same time over the loss of her pregnancy, the loss of the business and the climbing accident were all now far enough in the past that they could be referenced without reigniting further discontent. She could see how they had experienced their share of enough chaos.

"At the time I was hurting, and I know you were too. The idea of another baby being born was like a hope for finding the painkiller to a migraine that wouldn't dissipate. After that pain was in the past though, watching our two babies grow up to become adults has been the most satisfying thing I have ever experienced." She turned to look at Kevin for what she would say next. "We have two wonderful kids, and now one of them is starting a family of her own. You have been a great father Kevin. I just want you to know that."

Letting the statement sink in for a moment, Kevin turned to make eye contact with her and said, "Thank you, Jenny. I always thought you knew you were a great mom, and I have said it from time to time but I know that both Mella and Daniel think of you as a superhero." Jenny gave Kevin a satisfied smile with a sleepy look on her face.

Jenny was exhausted and had slept very poorly on the cot in the hospital room with Mella. Her eyelids were already showing their heaviness and after a few more breaths Jenny's face had relaxed and she fell into a deep and restful sleep.

Kevin lay there thinking about past conversations with her. Jenny always wanted to spend more time together with Kevin, because for her, time spent together was the most important measure of their bond. But it seemed like neither of them could go for very long without a project or work deadline to keep their minds active.

Maybe seeing what Mella went through and relating it to their early struggles would help them both let go of that need to stay busy all of the time, instead of unconsciously holding onto the seed of lingering fear which was planted when they went through their earlier time of losses. They were now financially secure and could shift their attention over to guiding other people rather than doing everything themselves. They could be comfortable having their "noses in but fingers out," as one of Kevin's board members would say when it came to mentoring others.

Jenny was set to retire from the leading executive position at the hospital in a year. When she was down to a more manageable part-time commitment of a board role maybe it would be time for him to complete a transition process too. Thinking about how that might work reminded him of the journey he had already taken.

Kevin had become a CEO again, this time it was for a new housing fund he had founded. He had gone back to Paul Wright, who had become a good friend, and the network he had built starting with the initial contacts from the Cancer Foundation Gala event and Paul's introductions. The group funded many homes and then after connecting with three large companies which were building thousands of houses and condos each year, Kevin formed alliances that had allowed them to grow their housing portfolio faster than any of the other existing publicly traded real estate funds. Investment professionals had enough experience now to see how the Shared Equity programs worked and the publicly traded real estate funds with Shared

Equity portfolios had become nearly universal investment holdings for all pension plans.

Kevin had taken the idea of Shared Equity Housing to the government housing associations and major real estate funds across the country. The markets officially came to recognize the gargantuan value of equity in the housing markets. When that happened, governments and major financial services companies began precisely tracking the equity value in housing independently from the mortgage market. As the housing markets continued to expand and become more sensitive to interest rate changes, policymakers now watched the housing funds' share prices as closely as housing starts to provide another leading indicator for the economy.

Shared Equity financial products had become more sophisticated. They now offered different combinations of equity coupled with transitional mortgage options to compete with the other housing funds that were sprouting up all over the country. Kevin's company offered some of the most advanced options in the marketplace, which were made easier to administer because of the software they now had which was fully automated by artificial intelligence. A.I. helped them facilitate all transactions as well as monitor data on real estate markets, population growth, and migration giving them the ability to predict the exact homes to buy and the price to pay for them. The decision-making tools were far better than any human mind could synthesize. It was scary how accurate they were.

Kevin still privately held a small portfolio of homes that he had invested in personally using the Shared Equity approach. He liked being in direct contact with families to see first hand how they were handling the process, and to stay aware of any changes in the marketplace or advances by their competitors.

Before resigning to the weight of his own eyelids, Kevin thought that it could be possible to shift his leadership role over the next year to give him more time with Jenny. He decided to start planning for it to consider what it would take for him to become comfortable with the idea.

*****

Kevin went into the office the next day with Jenny sleeping in to catch up on all the sleep she'd missed. Mella's baby was successfully putting on weight and had grown out of the respirator. Her husband Mark was an attentive and devoted father, which gave both Jenny and Kevin peace of mind knowing the baby would be well looked after. He thought about Mella for a moment and how she had her own family now. The 'Evans' he thought to himself and remembered when Mella was a baby herself. It was just her and Jennifer and him in their first house, the one that had been his first rental property. Now Mella was in her own home, one that he had helped her and Mark with a downpayment for. He had helped his son Daniel too, but he was still a bachelor so a condo seemed like the right place for Danny to start.

He hadn't funded his kids' homes through the company though. He had accumulated enough wealth over the years to do it personally, and it was simpler that way versus having to deal with the family conflict-of-interest issues that would be created because he was the CEO and the company was publicly traded. It was so much easier for people now, he thought, looking back to his experience after selling the home they had built themselves which was over-leveraged at the time, and how hard it had been to get back into the market.

Mella and Mark had decent income for their ages so they were able to get a mortgage easily with the amount of downpayment they started with. Mark was an engineer who happened to be extremely patient so he got along better with Mella than any of them. Mella had followed through with her desire to tackle human rights issues by getting a law degree. She not only worked on international NGO policies but also handled whistleblower litigation within the firm she joined out of university.

Things had certainly changed. After swapping out her courses and getting back on campus near the end of her freshman year at university, Mella had expressed no intention of moving back home even in the summer breaks between terms. She was happier as an adult with independence and control of her schedule, far more than she had ever been growing up. When Daniel moved out to go to college the year after Max had died, he and Jenny realized they didn't need as much space. It was hard to let go of the house though. He and Jenny had toured some condos and townhouses and thought that it would be nice not to have to look after as much yard or interior space but they just couldn't relinquish the idea of having their own nicely designed home. They had seen what they could do with some imagination and were in a much better place financially.

It was just five years earlier that they had found the "little cottage on the water," which is what they had called it. There was an area along the waterfront where the lots were quite narrow because the row of homes built there originally was meant to be summer getaways. Over time as the city had grown out around them, they were demolished and new architectural masterpieces were built in their place. The shoreline was a little rocky in most places but on a small strip of sandy beach, there was one old remaining cottage from the '60s.

Kevin's company was growing by leaps and bounds at that time and Jennifer had built up a secure pension within the hospital's pension plan, so with some of the proceeds from the shared equity homes that had eventually been sold to the occupants, they realized they could buy the cottage and take the time to create a spectacular design for a home they could retire into. They had to pay more than the asking price for an old vintage cabin to make sure they were the winning bidder but looking back on that decision, it was clear the extra money they had paid for the location provided a positive "return on investment," that couldn't be measured.

The time they'd spent together coming up with the perfect design for that site brought back all of the happy memories of their first dream home. The many enjoyable evenings looking over architectural books, drinking wine with a new appreciation for its flavour, and dreaming of all of the little details they would put into the design of the new home reformed the bond that had brought them together originally. This time having it built was no big deal. They had no deadline to move, no financial pressure, and no kids to worry about trying to account for in the design. They paid a little more on the move when it was finally done, but they hardly had to lift a finger. Three years to the day from when they closed on the purchase of the lot with the cottage, they had their first night's sleep in the new home. They were by themselves, but had been so energized by the move that they couldn't keep their hands to themselves, when they finally lay down in bed.

They still didn't have all the sheets and bedding unpacked but made love just the same. With a single sheet and blanket on the bed that night, it had felt like they were back in the days after university when they only had simple furnishings in their home.

Walking around the home that next morning, a serene sense of peace had enveloped Kevin's mind. It was during the balmy weeks in the summer when the housing market wasn't usually very active and the craziness at the Hospital had subsided for a moment so Jenny could relax too. Remembering looking out at the breathtaking view of the water and with him sipping his rooibos tea and Jenny with her latte, it was like the sun stopped moving through the sky and the waves were just an image on a painting. He thought about his walk around the home after that for another inspection, not that anything needed to be done, but just to take in all of the finishing touches. Kevin remembered admiring the hardscape concrete tiles and polished pebble stones around the tree beds. Glancing at the custom metal and wood panelling that covered the exterior of the home and the way the light reflected off the different surfaces, he thought that it was a work of art. He knew he wouldn't have to worry about yard maintenance here fortunately. The house took up so much of the lot from side to side they could have a company take care of the yard once every two weeks for an hour and it would be kept in perfect condition all year long.

The inside of the home was an architectural masterpiece. The design team working on the plans for the home coordinated all of the room layout details with an interior design firm that had plenty of experience with custom woodwork and exotic furniture procurement. Thought went into the elements of each room including the angle of exposure to the sun for how the light was cast across the interior spaces throughout the day. The home made them feel as if they were standing a little taller and breathing a little deeper since moving in. That first morning waking up in their new home was one of his favourite new memories and now he got to live out that same meditative experience every day.

Shaking his head out of the daydream Kevin looked back down at his desk so he could review the latest performance numbers displayed on the screen. It was a compilation of all the scores he liked to keep tabs on for the company and the housing market.

The portion of the overall population that now owned their homes, including people who were at varying stages in a Shared Equity Housing program, was no longer at the "prehistoric" level of 67% where it was when Paul Wright had funded the first Shared Equity homes. When Kevin's housing company first got started the year after Max died, there were only tens of thousands of people starting to build equity with various real estate funds running different versions of the program. Now, it was mind-numbing to think that millions of families were living in Shared Equity homes, benefiting from John Nash's "beautiful mind" and his discovery of the existence of optimal sharing agreements he called points of equilibrium.

Now the homeownership level was threatening to break 90%. Which is what Max had found in Singapore when travelling back in the early 2000s. The fact that Shared Equity programs were now working in larger countries around the globe, as companies in different countries started appearing, was amazing to see.

With the homeownership level as high as it was, people could now see that it was possible in a lifetime for virtually everyone in the country to be able to own a home and eventually pay off the mortgage, making it far easier for them in retirement. The equity that this generation was building up would help springboard the next generation into getting started sooner.

This was a vast improvement over the situation when Kevin was looking to get his family back into the housing market. It is astounding how much economic growth could occur given enough time.

While scrolling down the list of scores on his report, a message notification came up on the screen.

"From Simon Hunt?" Kevin said aloud to himself. "It has been a long time since I have heard from you," he thought.

When Kevin opened up the message it was an excerpt from the obituary for Ralph Heinz with a link to the full write up.

"What?!" Kevin said aloud in his office. Kevin then held his breath for a moment while he read through the first few sentences again until he was satisfied he understood what he was seeing.

The write up said that Ralph had died of natural causes at the age of 84. It went on to say that he was survived by his three daughters and seven grandchildren. It made mention of his long business career and that he had never stopped being actively involved in his companies. The obituary finished with a statement that didn't mention a funeral but said that Ralph was cremated and his ashes were spread with his family present in the countryside near the small town where he grew up.

The chain of memories from the events that started 22 years prior when Ralph had triggered the shotgun clause washed over him and after a moment of tension reliving those experiences it felt like those thoughts of uncertainty finally receded away from the shoreline of his consciousness, never to return.

*****

Kevin would later find out from Simon, who had kept closer tabs on Ralph, that a private equity group had bought out all of Ralph's company holdings and given Ralph an honorary board seat as one of Ralph's conditions of selling. Apparently some friction developed shortly after the companies were sold and Ralph was asked to step off the board three months later because of some aggressive accounting practices that had been used. After that the private equity firm wanted a fresh start. All of the companies were renamed and given new logos designed to modernize their image. Ralph's work in building up these fairly generic businesses now amounted to the proceeds of the sale. Money from the proceeds was spread into common diversified investments that would be divided amongst his daughters presumably. Nothing from what Ralph had worked on his whole life would be recognizable within a year of his death.

Curled up, sitting next to each other on the couch that night, Jenny and Kevin enjoyed warm drinks and the view out over the water. Kevin decided to mention the news, "I heard from Simon Hunt today."

"Oh yeah? The guy you worked with at the old software company?" Jenny vaguely remembered.

"Right. He sent me a message with the obituary for Ralph Heinz," Kevin said with a tone Jenny took as indifference, rather than a hint of sympathy she would have expected.

"Who was that?" Jenny didn't realize the connection.

"Ralph was the guy that triggered the shotgun clause originally, when we mortgaged the house," Kevin clarified.

"Oh. Did you ever see him after that?"

"Oddly no. But I had to read it twice before I would let myself believe it. I don't know why this came to mind but Ralph being gone made me think that enough time has passed that my old ghosts may finally be put to rest." Kevin sighed quietly and relaxed when he said it.

Chapter 12
GROWING FAMILY

A couple of weeks after Mella came home from the hospital with her baby girl, Jenny and Kevin went out for dinner with Paul Wright and his wife Angela at their favourite restaurant. Jenny was the first to share some big news. After the recent scare with Mella, their son the bachelor had told them he was shopping for an engagement ring. Daniel called them last night to say that his girlfriend had accepted his proposal and they were now engaged to be married. Congratulations and more wine was shared and the two couples went on to have a great time enjoying a fantastic meal. The head chef had changed three years ago at the Fig Tree Bistro, but it still had some of the best Italian dishes in the city. During part of the conversation they got to hear Angela tell them about all of her and Paul's favourite travel destinations. There were stories of dozens of hotspots around the world that were accumulated with their frequent travel activity over the last 10 years.

After dinner, Kevin and Jenny agreed they would have a short vacation to Victoria, British Columbia. Angela and Paul described it and the surrounding islands like a pristine showcase of the West Coast. They said that on the middle of the island where the city of Victoria is located there were rocky mountains like the Swiss alps, but were largely kept secret from the rest of the world. Angela raved about the exhilarating helicopter tour they had taken into the mountains for a short day trip. Kevin was surprised he had never heard of the Strathcona Park mountains with all of his past climbing experience. Angela described Victoria as having the most comfortable summer weather even with the effects of climate change being felt across North America. Plus, they saw orca whales and had amazing food that now grew in the ocean water within protected inlets and bays around the island. Kevin thought It sounded like a great place to start their more relaxed lifestyle.

*****

After a few weeks of thinking, and starting to plan out what a transition of leadership would look like, Kevin decided he didn't want to hold onto his personal portfolio of homes. Instead he would split them up and sell one third each to three different funds so that he didn't have what Max would say was a fragile financial position, being dependent on the management team of any one company to do everything right. He had a great team of people leading at the top of different divisions of his company and could easily see his current number two stepping up to take over his position as CEO. He would ultimately step back and remain a member of the board of directors. But that didn't feel like it would be the complete solution for him going forward.

Kevin recently heard it said that 'we all die twice.' We die once when the blood stops flowing in our veins and our eyes close for the last time. The second time we die is when our name is mentioned for the last time aloud or in print, for the kind of mark we left on the world while we were alive.

It made Kevin think about the endless number of times he had questioned the meaning for his life. Not life in general, but what his life's specific purpose should be. He never found it satisfying to think about it like Ralph had, remembering how Ralph used to talk when he had first invested in his original software company, "just making money as a way to keep score." It was clear that what Ralph left to his family in substantial monetary inheritance would be distributed amongst the relatives, but Ralph's name would be forgotten from the business world within a few years. His companies were competitive in the market but they would be traded many times over or split up by the private equity funds to capture more financial value, while Ralph's descendants would keep their money in less management-intensive investments.

When Kevin thought about Jenny's or his legacies, it occurred to him that they had both been working at purposes that brought their family financial benefit but also had a positive impact on those around them.

Jenny's management of the hospital and her work with the hospital foundation had led to one of their most successful fundraising campaigns ever. Because the majority of the donations didn't come from any one particular person, the board decided to name the neonatal wing of the hospital "The Jennifer Robertson New Family Centre." The board surprised her at the quarterly meeting following the completion of the fund raising campaign. It was a joyously tearful day when the groundbreaking dedication took place and they officially announced it to the hospital staff, general public, and media.

Kevin wasn't one who desired any personal attention from the press so his legacy would have to be one that measured up to his internal standards. He was thinking that he would spend more time when he retired working as a diplomat to meet with Ministers of Finance or other similarly appointed people in other countries. He and his team would work with them as advisors to help them integrate new funding options for housing into their existing national housing finance systems.

He and Jenny would never have issues with generating income or holding onto enough equity now for their "retirement" years, which he guessed wouldn't see them ever fully stopping all productive work.

As the world population continued towards 11 billion people and the major urban centres in every country were becoming more densely populated, the cost of housing continued to rise. Programs like the Shared Equity Housing model were not only necessary, but they irrefutably proved to be great investments. Both parties grew their equity successfully — the investor "sharer" and the family living in the home receiving the share. Housing as an asset class had proven that it was exceptionally well hedged against inflation.

One quote that Kevin thought fit well for what happened with the value of real estate over time was: "People overestimate growth in the short term, but they underestimate growth in the long term." He could see how much the statement was true, thinking back to the value of homes in the 1950s when the grandmother in Max's story saved up enough to buy that first home for $11,000.

Upon further reflection of that quote, Kevin thought that it was not only true in the financial sense, but also applied to the strength of the bond in a relationship.

Kevin could see that wherever he had built his business relationships on the basis that he would work with those people for the long-term, they had the most trust. Maybe that would turn out to be true for him and Jenny too.

Kevin had changed over the years to support building stronger relationships. It had required that he try to see things from another person's point of view, compromise more often, and make decisions on what would maintain a relationship rather than only always try to win an argument. He realized, no matter how much he thought he was right, people experienced mental blind spots and suffered from biases which meant he could be wrong just as often.

The clearest decision Kevin knew he could make as an act of love for Jenny, was to give her his time first. He realized that it would be a great adventure to go and see more of the world with her. Along the way once in a while they could stop in and see the housing developers in parts of the world still catching up with the Shared Equity Housing approach. Jenny would also want to visit health clinics in different parts of the world to connect them with the international foundations she was aware of. It would be a great way for them to keep their minds active while meeting new people and exploring beautiful places around the globe.

*****

In the months leading up to Jennifer and Kevin officially passing their respective batons, they decided to go for a weekend holiday to Victoria, B.C. and book themselves onto a whale watching tour. After getting settled the morning they arrived they made their way down to the docks to get ready for their powerboat tour. Right on schedule as if it was a show at SeaWorld, the tour boat came upon a pod of orcas inside the channel between two islands. It was nature at its finest. These smooth glistening creatures looked like they were wearing tuxedos while they arched up and out of the water, swimming along ahead of the boat. When the boat stopped to turn around, one of the orcas breached and then came out of the water again right up into the air, nearly carrying the full weight of its body clear of the surface. When it slammed back down there was a perfect rooster tail splash in both directions away from its body, spraying water 10 feet up in the air. The pod they saw had five whales in total but two of them seemed much smaller than the other three. The tour guide said they would have been born within the last year. The sun was shining bright but the experience gave them both the shivers.

They went out for dinner after sunset that night at a restaurant by Victoria's "inner harbour," a waterway encircled on three sides by heritage buildings. One of those landmarks being the original stone parliamentary building which was lit up on all edges and corners by strings of white lights. After dinner, they went back to where they were staying at the historic Empress Hotel overlooking the harbour. It was in near-mint condition following its recent renovation, which was the fourth time it had been refinished in its history. Their experience in Victoria was one of the most romantic adventures of their lives. The next morning they went down for their appointment to have a massage which was followed by a sauna to fully relax. After going up to their room to freshen up before lunch, with the mid morning sun streaming in through the windows they procrastinated getting into the shower and ended up in bed and made love.

It was delicious.

"It looks like we may be late for our lunch reservation," Jenny said with a smile.

"It's not your fault. I think you were distracted," Kevin responded coyly, stroking Jenny's shoulder.

"Oh I was distracted was I?" Jenny shoved Kevin's chest.

Kevin never imagined they would be more head-over-heels for each other on the verge of their 60th birthdays than they had been in their early twenties. Then again, so much of what had happened in their lives wouldn't have been imaginable when they first married.

This weekend vacationing with Jennifer had filled Kevin up with power. It was a kind of enduring energy that would keep him going. It came with a sense of certainty and belief that a more resilient force was keeping them together. They were both passionate about their work which compelled them forward but he now knew they could persist through anything they would face in the future. They didn't talk about those things. It was always harder to put those feelings into words and adequately describe them. So, it took them time, and by watching one another's body language and facial expressions, they eventually understood what the other meant. That understanding was more than one could get from listening alone because it involved consistent action observed over days, weeks, months.

They had endured loss together and gone on to create not only a new dream home but communities of people that would sustain their dreams at work. After all of the experiences they'd shared Kevin arrived at an undeniable conclusion. He knew they would survive together, and he could never be convinced otherwise.

But then Jennifer surprised him by saying something out loud he never expected to hear.

"Thanks for bringing me back to the afternoon on the pebble sand beach, Kevin. It's exactly as I remember it. Perfect in every way."

The End

Notes For Chapter 6

(1) Michael Porter's Creating Shared Value (CSV)
     business concept is described on this Wikipedia
     page: https://en.wikipedia.org/wiki/
     Creating_shared_value

     The Case for Letting Business Solve Social
     Problems TED Talk: https://www.ted.com/talks/
     michael_porter_the_case_for_letting_business_sol
     ve_social_problems?language=en

(2) https://www.statista.com/statistics/184902/
     homeownership-rate-in-the-us-since-2003/

(3) https://www.theglobeandmail.com/report-on-
     business/economy/foreclosures-in-us-surge-to-
     record-high/article1211177/

(4) http://www.abeautifulmind.com/a-beautiful-mind-
     film/

(5) For a house worth $500,000 that is rented,
     property management costs could be between
     $200-$240 per month, the cost of vacancy could
     average between $180 and $215 per month, and the
     average monthly maintenance cost and capital
     reserve could be $375 to $430 per month, adding
     up to a total cost of $755 to $885 per month.

For a bank that has an 80% loan to value mortgage on the same property totalling $400,000, the mortgage servicing cost would be $60 to $74 per month. The lender's cost of looking after a loan on an owner occupied home is 1/10th of what it costs a landlord to look after a rented property.

(6)   The historical vacancy rate of rented homes has averaged 7.5% and the historical vacancy rate of owned homes has averaged 1.5%. The difference in vacancy could be contributed to the need for people to sell their home before they buy a new one and move. By using a Shared Equity agreement it can be forecasted that a large portfolio of homes could see its vacancy rate reduced by 6% on average over time.

(7)   With a Shared Equity Housing agreement improving cash flow in residential real estate investment assets, the targeted selection of homes can focus on higher quality, newer properties in better locations. Taking into account the pride of ownership and improved maintenance of a Shared Equity home compared to regular rental investments, the growth in value for a Shared Equity Housing investment has the potential to increase faster than older rental properties with fewer years left in their economic life span.

Bibliography

Boleat, Mark. *National Housing Finance Systems: A Comparative Study.* Croom Helm. 1985.

Colquitt, Joetta. *Credit Risk Management: How to Avoid Lending Disasters and Maximize Earnings.* McGraw-Hill. 2007.

Davidson, James Dale and Rees-Mogg, Lord William. *The Sovereign Individual: Mastering the Transition to the Information Age.* Touchstone. 1997.

Evans, Alan W. *Economics, Real Estate & The Supply of Land.* Blackwell Publishing. 2004.

Graeber, David. *Debt: The First 5000 Years.* Melville House Publishing. 2011.

Homer, Sidney. *A History of Interest Rates: 2000 B.C. to the Present.* Rutgers University Press. 1963.

Krakauer, Jon. *Eiger Dreams: Ventures Among Men and Mountains.* First Anchor Books. 1997.

Mian, Atif and Sufi, Amir. *House of Debt: How They (and You) Caused the Great Recession, And How We Can Prevent It From Happening Again.* The University of Chicago Press. 2014.

Mishkin, Frederic S. And Serletis, Apostolos. *The Economics of Money, Banking, and Financial Markets.* Pearson Addison Wesley. 2001.

Nash, John. *Equilibrium Points in n-Person Games.*
Proceedings of the National Academy of Sciences
of the United States of America, Vol. 36, No. 1 (Jan.
15, 1950), pp. 48-49.

Nash, John. *The Bargaining Problem.* Econometrica Vol.
18, No. 2, (April 1950), pp.155-162.

Nash, John. *Non-Cooperative Games.* The Annals of
Mathematics, Second Series, Vol. 54, No. 2, (Sep.,
1951). pp. 286-295.

Nash, John. *Two Person Cooperative Games.* Econometrica
Vol. 21, No. 1, (Jan. 1953), pp. 128-140.

O'Flaherty, Brendan. *City Economics.* Harvard University
Press. 2005.

Rowbotham, Michael. *The Grip of Death: A Study of
Modern Money, Debt Slavery and Destructive Economics.*
Jon Carpenter Publishing. 1998.

Saunders, Anthony and Thomas, Hugh. *Financial
Institutions Management.* McGraw-Hill Ryerson. 1997.

Schiller, Robert J. *Irrational Exuberance, Revised and
Expanded Third Edition.* Princeton University Press.
2015

Schiller, Robert J. *The New Financial Order: Risk in the
21st Century.* Princeton University Press. 2003.

Schiller, Robert J. *Macro Markets: Creating Institutions for Managing Society's Largest Economic Risks.* Oxford University Press Inc. 1993.

Shapiro, Alan C. *Multinational Financial Management.* John Wiley & Sons. 2006.

Smith, Adam. *The Wealth of Nations.* Bantam Classic Edition. 2003. Originally Published in 1776.

Soto, Hernando De. *The Mystery of Capital: Why Capitalism Triumphs in the West and Fails Everywhere Else.* Basic Books. 2000.

Taleb, Nassim Nicholas. *AntiFragile: Things That Gain From Disorder.* Random House. Nov. 27, 2012.

Vaillant, George E. *Triumphs of Experience - The Men of the Harvard Grant Study.* First Harvard University Press , 2012.

Yew, Lee Kuan. *From Third World to First: The Singapore Story 1965-2000.* HarperCollins. 2000.

Inflation data from https://www.inflation.eu and https://tradingeconomics.com/country-list/inflation-rate